LUNAR

ACCORD

CHELSEA McDONALD

PLAYLIST

Mr. Saxobeat (*by Alexandra Stan*)

Dark Paradise (*by Lana Del Rey*)

Keeping Your Head Up (*by Birdy*)

I See Fire (*by Ed Sheeran*)

In an Instant (*by Tina*)

So Sick (*by Ne-Yo*)

Undercover (*by Kehlani*)

Open up The Sky (*by Sam Tsui*)

Company (*by Justin Bieber*)

Save It Til Morning (*by Fergie*)

Wonderland (*by Natalia Kills*)

You (*by Nathaniel*)

Distance (*by Omarion*)

Dead In the Water (*by Ellie Goulding*)

Eyes Wide Shut (*by JLS*)

"Fantasy is a necessary ingredient in living, it's a way of looking at life through the wrong end of the telescope."

- Dr. Seuss

PROLOGUE

I ONCE SAID I WOULDN'T TRADE him or our life together for anything. I was wrong. In that moment, I couldn't have disagreed with myself more.

CHAPTER ONE

IT WAS SUCH A BEAUTIFUL day outside, I wish I had of taken my lunch and sat in the courtyard. *Oh, well.*

This was it. My last day of college studying for my nursing degree. In a few months I would be starting my full time Alpha training. That thought excited me beyond belief. I had only continued my studies so that I could feel useful in situations outside of being an Alpha.

I can't wait, I thought to myself. I desperately wanted to be rid of this place. As I walked past the noisy cafeteria, I could only imagine the goings on inside. Boys swinging on chairs throwing footballs, girls gossiping and cheering; all my classmates were always so loud and boisterous. It was almost like I hadn't left high school sometimes.

I couldn't expect much else from a university that was made up of over sixty percent Lycan kind I suppose. I couldn't be too harsh on my classmates, and I was definitely not complaining about my experience there. I was just all too ready for a dramatic change in my life. College had been good to me; I wasn't a loser or an outcast. I mainly kept to myself and tried to push through my studies as quickly as I could.

Another reason I couldn't wait to get out of college was due to the fact that I was the Alpha's daughter. Back in high school I didn't especially notice how everyone treated me, because I was with my friends all the time just having a good time.

Now in college, it was lonelier. All my friends were off doing other things. That's how I noticed the way the pack members were so different around me. Parting in the halls for me, bowing their heads, saying my name, always smiling at me. Of course, that wasn't unusual behavior towards a future Alpha and I didn't fault them for it at all. It was just the magnitude of their respect that had startled me. I was treated like royalty but father said I'd get used to it over time.

I glanced at my watch. A little bit past two. My lunch break was almost over with only a few minutes to get back to class. After passing your exams and handing in your final lot of work, I didn't see the point in still attending classes; no one paid attention anyway. But, it was mostly last minute catch up work, discussing our results and talking about career pathways.

"Kira!" I heard my name being shouted as I walked out of my last class entering the courtyard, forever leaving the drab school building behind, to see my friend Carson waiting for me. She had agreed to meet me after my last class so we could walk into town together.

We'd known each other since high school and had been close ever since. Carson was one of the few who decided not to go to college. Instead she was chosen to train to be a pack warrior.

"Hey Carson. How was training today?" I called to her

as I rushed up to give her a hug. We'd both been busy the past couple of weeks with our commitments to meet up but we'd declared tonight an emergency movie night.

"Awesome, as per usual. I just love getting to watch Tyler while we're both technically working." She air-quoted and laughed. Tyler was Carson's mate. They had Imprinted each other shortly after she turned eighteen and it had all been smooth sailing from there.

A mate, or soulmate, was someone you were destined to be with, someone you're bonded to by the Moon Goddess. When a female Lycan hits the age of maturity between eighteen and twenty, was when they were supposed to find their mate.

Sometimes mates took longer to find because they lived far apart, so distance was a challenge. But some unlucky few don't find theirs, at all, with the amount of deaths due to pack wars or rogue attacks. Sadly, the few who don't find their soulmate slowly wither away and die, not being able to bear living life without their other half.

My eyes drifted down to the cracked pavement as I wallowed in my thoughts. I had turned twenty-two three months ago. I still hadn't found my mate, but I tried not to think too much about it because when I did, the prospect of being all alone and fading away was just too alarming.

Usually once a Lycan reaches maturity, they feel a pull, a need to start searching for their mate. It was quite normal for unmated Lycans to travel around other packs in search of their other half. If you felt the pull you were lucky. That meant your mate was close by; that you would find your special someone soon.

I had never felt that pull but I had always wondered what he would look like, what his name was, where out there he might be...

Carson's nudge in my side brought me back to the present and I gave her a small smile to thank her. I swear this girl knew me so well she could almost read my thoughts.

"He's out there, you know. You'll find him." She reassured me, looping her arm through mine we continued our walk into town.

"So, how was the last day of your school life? Do you feel accomplished yet?" She laughed as she mocked me. I used to say that I wouldn't feel like an adult until I had graduated college. Of course, this was years ago but she liked to remind me how naïve I was once upon a time.

"Completely boring!" I exclaimed as we entered the park and strolled down the path towards the library. "What an absolute waste of time, but hey! I'm free now so I couldn't care less."

"I know, right. Remember our last day of high school? How Mr. Wessel was droning on and on, but I actually felt sorry for him with the amount of ruckus our classmates were making." Carson said as we walked past the Town Hall and across Main Street to Sky's Treats bakery.

The little bell dinged above us as we stepped into the orange brick building and wandered up to the glass counter. With the afternoon sun streaming in through the windows, the place was as bright as Times Square.

The smells of chocolate and freshly baked cake slammed into me and I inhaled the deliciousness. I smiled as I saw our other friend Dante, behind the counter in her apron putting change in the cash register.

"Hey Dante!" I called as we reached the counter.

"Hey Kira, hey Carson." She said. "What can I get you guys?" She asked as we bent down and just about pressed our faces up against the glass case displaying all delicious, freshly made treats.

Dante's family had owned the bakery here in Albourne for generations and everything was always freshly made. Dante worked here whenever she wasn't at college getting her business degree.

I knew it sounded ridiculous but I had always secretly envied Dante. She had a typical pack life. She had a job and was working towards a college degree that she would actually get to put to use when she took over her family bakery.

Between my parents and the already hectic pace of my life I had never had a job. My father had just always said that learning to be the next pack leader was a hard-enough job as it was.

"I'll have a red velvet cupcake and a caramel macchiato." Carson ordered.

Hmm. I hesitated, weighing all of my options before deciding.

"I shall have a…blueberry scone with jam and cream, also a banana milkshake." I gave my order to Dante as Carson walked over and plopped down at a table near the window.

Dante went around the corner and told her mom, Allison, that we were here and that she was going for her break. I went to pay for our order but as Dante's mom comes to the till she waves me off.

"Alpha. It's on the house." She smiled and gave a small bow of her head, "I'm lucky that the business is doing well otherwise I'd have to close up shop with the amount of food you girls eat." She said with a laugh and a wide smile as she went about fixing our orders.

I walked to sit with Dante and Carson who were already chatting animatedly. I caught the end of what they are saying, something about a party. My phone beeped and I clicked to see I had received a message from Andrew, the only male in my pack that I'm close enough to call a friend.

'Party at mine tonight, 7pm. Be there or be a square ;)'

So, his parents had actually agreed to let him throw a party. I had heard that our Betas, his parents, Noah and Katherine were thinking about it but I didn't think that they'd allow it.

I tuned back into what the girls were saying and it seemed they were already picking out what they were wearing.

"I guess we're going then?" I asked rhetorically with a chuckle knowing that they couldn't miss a party.

Carson was a nightmare back in high school, she went to *all* of the parties whether she was invited or not. She'd calmed down a lot since she'd met Tyler, now that I thought about it.

Dante on the other hand, a few years younger than us, was a delicate flower but she'd go anywhere that we did, plus who wouldn't be up for having a good time with their friends.

"Woohoo!" Carson called. I guessed it was party time then.

As we left the bakery we all went our separate ways and agreed to meet at mine early on to get ready for the party together.

I was sat at our marble breakfast bar eating cereal and flipping through a magazine when my mother walked in with grocery bags filling both her hands.

"Need some help?" I laughed and stood up to help.

She looked around and took notice of me for the first time. "Oh, hi Kira. No, no you needn't bother."

She said as a large smile stretched upon her face. She immediately put the bags on the kitchen counter and came over to me.

She reached out and engulfed me in her arms for one of my mother's great bear hugs. Growing up in an Alpha household, and as the Alpha's daughter, was harder than it sounded and I was very grateful to have had my mother by my side throughout all the ups and downs. I thanked the Moon Goddess for giving her to me every day.

"How was your last day? Anything exciting happen today?" She began grilling me as we pulled away and she started going about the kitchen putting her shopping haul away.

I chuckled to myself, she'd asked me this same question nearly every day since I started elementary school. "Yeah! OMG, mom today the most amazing thing happened." I said in fake excitement.

"What? What happened? Tell me." She said rushing to stop what she was doing to hear all about my exciting news.

"Yeah, I finished university!" Her face went from an excited puppy to looking like I killed the cat. I burst out in laughter at the look on her face.

"Ha ha. Very funny Kira." She mocked and went back to putting everything away.

"How was your day, mother? What's happening in the life of our wonderful Luna?" I asked as I walked to the sink to wash my bowl out.

"Everything was great. Today I went to lunch with some of the girls, I did some errands for your father, and then I talked to your aunt Mary." She paused while reaching for the top shelf of the cupboard.

"Everyone says hello by the way." She continued as I walked back to my seat at the breakfast bar. I made a mental note to try and contact my family sometime soon. Had it really been that long since I last talked to my cousins?

I sat and watched her as she continued to babble on about her day and only the Goddess knew what else. I smiled at how animated she was while she was talking. As she came to a natural stop in her conversation, I jumped in. "Do you know when Dad will be home?"

"He said that he would, and I quote, 'be home before 6' but we both know how your father is, that man is just always losing track of time. So, we'll see." She said while pulling on her apron.

"Are you cooking tonight?" I asked, intrigued at what little slice of heaven she'd make for us tonight.

She made a noise of agreement while she started to collect some ingredients. "What would you like, chicken or beef?"

"Beef," I immediately spoke but then remembered I was going out and the girls would be here any minute.

"Dante and Carson are coming over soon, we'll be going over to Andrew's for the party tonight."

"I heard about that party. You'll make sure to be careful won't you dear?" She looked over at me with a stern expression on her face to which I replied with a simple nod of my head.

I almost laughed, I'm to be the next Alpha of the Silver pack. I would never do anything that I knew could jeopardize that, I had worked too hard already.

I'd been training to be the next pack leader all my life, I still remembered my first *official w*arrior training when I was just ten. It was horrible but I loved every second of earning my future title. Since then once a week my father would call me into his office to test me on everything from strategizing an attack to drilling me on the laws of our community.

It was no sooner than six o'clock when the girls were knocking down the door of our house.

"Kira. Carson and Dante are here." I heard my mother call up the stairs to me only a minute before they both rushed into my bedroom.

They squealed, dropping their things on the floor before Dante jumped on the bed next to me and Carson started rushing around the room in a blur.

"Kira! Come on. We only have an hour to get ready!" I turned to look at Dante and rolled my eyes as she let out a little giggle.

"She is such a drama queen." I whispered to Dante.

It wasn't until Carson started rifling through my closet that I panicked and rushed to get up. "Alright alright, just please don't hurt the clothes." I cried dramatically as she started throwing bits and pieces around.

She walked back out looking sheepish and mumbled a small, "sorry."

"What are you guys wearing tonight?" I asked as Carson took a seat in my armchair and Dante sat up to attention.

"Well! I've decided on that blue halter neck dress that I got the last time we went shopping." Carson said.

"Nice," I remembered that dress, it looked gorgeous on her especially because of how the color was only slightly darker than her big blue eyes.

"And I will be wearing my jeans and sneakers." As per the usual Dante, I smiled at my friend as Carson scoffed. Carson was what you would call a fashionista, or so she liked to think anyway. She'd always be in the shortest dresses, the tightest jeans and the highest heels. She never approved of what we wore because we've got a more laid back style. I wasn't trying to actively seek attention; I just want to have a good time.

I walked into my closet trying to think of what I'd wear, "Any suggestions on what I should wear?"

My closet wasn't massive but I did have a wide variety of clothes from formal dresses to jogging bottoms, and nearly everything in between.

"Something sparkly." I heard Dante yell.

"Something tight." I heard Carson call.

My belly laugh boomed from the closet as I could hear them start to argue over what I'd wear. So, something tight *and* sparkly.

I grabbed a long sleeve pink lace top, some black, ripped skinny jeans and a sweetheart bandeau. I walked into the doorway of my en-suite bathroom and turned to my friends, "Ready, set… Go!"

I locked the bathroom door behind me as a whirlwind of commotion sounded on the other side. I chuckled to myself as I turned on the shower and started to strip off my clothes.

With me, Carson and Dante it had always been a competition to see who'd get ready the quickest. My mother always laughed but the game could get pretty intense.

I hopped into the shower quickly, not bothering to wash my hair. I shut the shower off after ridding myself of all the shower gel suds and towel dried myself. I heard my stereo blasting some Chris Brown and started humming and singing along. I slipped on my robe and over the next twenty minutes I moisturized, applied the slightest of make-up; mainly to my eyes, then untangled and straightened my hair.

As I stared at my reflection in the mirror I couldn't help but admire how much I looked like my mother. Apart from my naturally dark hair, from my father, I could've been the spitting image. I had her caramel brown eyes, her nose and even her beautifully long lashes. I had truly been blessed, I had a gorgeous mother and a strong protective father.

Finally, after I shrunk my ego down, I slid on my clothes and walked back into my bedroom. Carson was sat at my vanity putting the finishing touches on her hair and makeup while Dante was on the bed doing the funniest pants dance I had ever seen.

"You look really nice Kira," Dante smiled as I lifted up my shoes to show her the sparkly-ness of my outfit.

"Tight *and* sparkly." I said as Carson grinned in the mirror and I did a little twirl for dramatic effect.

"DAMN GURL. I'd tap that," We all burst out laughing at Carson's' comment.

I heard a knock on my bedroom door as we calmed ourselves down, "Come in."

"Hiya girls, I don't want to interrupt but your mother sent these up." My father entered with a plate of what looked like my mother's' famous mint chocolate brownies.

"Hiya Daddy." I smiled and gave him a peck on the cheek as I took the plate from him.

After getting ready we sat around my room chatting, listening to music and planning our summer activities. Dante and I were no longer studying so that meant that we had some major free time over the next couple of months.

"Girls!" I heard my mother shout, "Tyler is here to pick you up." And just like that we made our way downstairs to begin our night.

My mother and father were huddled at the door with a spiffed-up Tyler.

"Hey Tyler." Dante and I said as Carson walked up and grabbed his hand giving him a big lovesick grin.

"Goodnight Alpha, Luna." Carson and Tyler said to my parents as they walked out.

"Awesome brownies as per usual Mrs. B." Dante said and I nodded along in agreement, "Thanks mom!"

"Save me some leftovers, pleaseeeee." I pleaded to my mother as Dante pushed me out the door following in our friends' wake.

"You all have fun tonight," My mother said behind us.

"And be safe honey!" I heard dad shout as we got further away from the house.

"Bye!" We shouted giggling as we tried to catch up to our loved-up friends.

The closer we walked to Andrews' street the louder the music got and the more people we could see. As we made our way up the small driveway and into the house I stopped to greet a few people along the way.

A grin stretched across my face as I heard Wynter Gordon already booming through Andrews sound system.

As soon as we stepped through the doorway all that I could see while looking around was people everywhere. It didn't look like anybody was too drunk yet, nobody was dancing on the tables yet at least. Plus, it still smelled like perfume and beer so that was a good sign.

Girls were glad in beautiful dresses, revealing skirts and stiletto heels. *Ouch*. Guys were hanging about with cups in their hands, girls on their arms and smiles on their faces. It brought a smile to my face to see Lycans of all ages and backgrounds socializing.

As I made my way into the living room with Dante, Carson shouted "We're off to explore." And just like that our group was made a duo. I noticed that most of the furniture had been either removed or pushed against the walls, and I took note of the ping pong table in the dining room not being used. *Yet.*

Andrew came bounding up to us as we made our way deeper into the living room. With two drinks in his hand he greeted us, "Hello ladies."

He handed us the drinks and I took a big whiff before deciding it was okay and had a sip.

"It's Vodka and Coke," Andrew answered with a bright smile to an unsure looking Dante before he too disappeared into the crowd. I had to admit the parties that Andrew threw were known to be quite good. Flashing colored lights were everywhere, fire pits out on the patio and some killer music.

We were dancing outside on the back patio when we finally spotted Carson again, Tyler nowhere to be seen, an hour or so later. Carson came to join us with three shots in one hand and a cup in the other. She handed us each one shot and then started counting down.

"…1." We all downed the shot as the song morphed into Mr. Saxobeat.

Hmm, Strawberry milk.

"That was awesome! What was that?" I just about shouted over at Carson.

"Tequila."

Alcohol had a weakened effect on Lycans, however I was beginning to feel a bit buzzed. That's one of the reasons I let myself loose when I did come to parties, it was very hard for us to get out of control.

As the hours flew past the drinks kept coming, everything from Vodka to Wine. We danced together and even with some of the guys in the pack.

After a while Tyler found his way to us and attached himself to Carson as they both danced to the music. I loved the energy at parties, everyone was just having fun and dancing along to everything.

Not long after, Andrew came over to join our little group and started goofily dancing between me and Dante.

"I'll get the drinks this time," I shouted after finishing

my, *fifteenth?* drink leaving them as I walked through the pumping crowd. As I kept bumping into people I realized that maybe I was too much of a lightweight for any more drinks.

I shrugged off my incoherent thoughts and lazily swayed my hips humming along to one of Pitbull's songs as I made my way back into the kitchen. I looked at all the bottles of liquor on the counter but couldn't quite recognize what was what.

When I spotted a green glass bottle I guessed it to be Midori and moved to pick it up. I poured out our drinks but hung back to pour an extra shot for myself. I threw back my shot and looked around the room at all my pack mates having a good time.

I tried to pick up the cups but struggled with all five of them. I grabbed four with my hands then bent down to pick up the fifth one between my teeth. I ignored my inner rational thoughts as I tried to turn as slowly as I could towards the door.

Just as I thought I was clear I felt a warm tingle on my elbow and gasped dropping my cup. My drink splashed in a puddle at my feet, I was too far gone to care about my shoes but I groaned at the sad loss of my drink. I shifted to look at who was responsible and froze on the spot. *Holy hell!*

CHAPTER TWO

THE MOMENT I LOOKED INTO his eyes I knew that I was in trouble. My inner beast howled and yipped for joy knowing she wouldn't be alone ever again. She had just imprinted on her mate.

Imprinting on your mate was the first stage in the mating process. Imprinting just meant seeing your mate for the first time and recognizing each other as soulmates mates. The next stages were the marking, and then the mating but Alpha couples usually had a ceremony before marking each other for eternity, to introduce the mates to the pack.

I realized I'd frozen on the spot in the middle of a very hectic party, "Don't. Move. I'll be back in a second." I squinted my eyes in a glare to make sure I got my point across.

Rushing out the back door I tried to clear my mind but it was too fuzzy from the alcohol and I was just about freaking the fuck out. I handed the drinks out to my friends, "Where's yours?" Andrew asked.

"I spilt a little. I'll be back later," I smiled as my friends easily let me leave.

I returned to my previous spot in the kitchen, once again frozen in front of my mate. I stared. I was always taught that it was rude to stare but at this moment in time I just didn't seem capable to do anything but stare. He seemed older than I was, and taller.

"Mate." His voice a husky growl. "I'm Asher."

His facial features were defined but to the brink of looking too thin. He had shaggy light brown hair, he had a bit of a beard and the most beautiful hazel eyes to stare back at me.

"Kira," I said when I finally find my voice. My eyes slowly roamed down his body; his chest, his torso, where I knew he'd be hiding some muscle, and his well-toned arms.

I brought my eyes back up to his and smiled in a daze. *This is my mate.* My inner beast had practically melted into a puddle at her mate's feet.

Everything happened so quickly but I saw it happening, he leaned in and paused a breath away from me. His eyes flickered to my lips and I realized that he'd shifted to trap me between him and the kitchen bench.

Suddenly, I felt extremely nervous. Of course, it wasn't my first kiss but it felt like it was. This was the kiss that would top all other kisses, forever. I steadied myself against the kitchen bench and waited in anticipation.

Our lips touched in a seemingly innocent kiss. It started out slow and steady but soon grew into something else, something more heated.

I pulled back briefly to prepare myself for another mind-blowing kiss and then crashed back into him, where he was ready and waiting. My hands moved from the bench behind me to the bottom of his shirt. Shakily they moved up his body and tangled themselves in his hair.

And that's how the rest of my night went. Kissing slowly turned into something more and continued until we were baring all in the middle of the forest. Our clothes disappeared as we took full advantage of the night.

How I got there, I didn't know. How many words were past between us, I didn't know. Did that bother me? I *really* didn't know. But, in that moment, I wanted desperately for him to make me his.

He was quick to lay me down. His kisses turned more ferocious as they travelled the length of my body. His raging hard on had been noticeable since we'd left the house but with a combination of the alcohol and the head rush I wasn't paying attention to how fast he was moving. Pulling my panties down my legs, his hands gripped my thighs.

His lips were still attached to mine as his fingers started to explore the space between my legs. His soft finger pads tingled as they teased me. I groaned and rocked my hips into his hand as his index finger plunged into my depths. I was ready when his hard cock eventually slammed into me. His movements had shocked my body as he broke through my virginity in one stoke. The sudden pain pulled tears from my eyes as I became more alert of the situation.

He began pounding into me and I looked to his face fazed by his hurried pace. I had to remind myself that this was the man I would spend forever with. I pushed the pain off as it being my first time. Of course, it wasn't how I'd thought my first time would be but I also hadn't thought I'd have to have waited this long.

The more my buzz wore off the more unsure I started to feel about all that was happening. I questioned whether I should have waited, if he'd see me differently for mating with him on the first night. But I was too far gone to realize that maybe I wasn't ready. I was too happy to be spending the night with my soulmate to care about my feelings or about what we were doing.

My beast had waited long enough, she needed this. The intimacy and connection that only mates shared, she had been so patient and so ready. This was my mate, my lover for eternity, what could possibly go wrong. I just couldn't help the nagging negativity in my heart that kept repeating itself over and over. *Don't trust whom you don't know...*

))))) (((((

It wasn't until the next day when I started to panic more heavily about the night before. I looked to my alarm clock to see it was only just past five am. It was too early.

After I'd mated with Asher last night we had said goodnight. He had promised that we would see each other today and then walked away. I went back to the party feeling like a walking contradiction, I was torn between my heart and my soul. I didn't stay long after that, I told the girls that I wasn't feeling well and was just going to head home. Guilt gnawed at me for not telling them the truth but my head was just too confused. What had made it worse was that the booze had completely worn off by the time I'd started walking home.

I just couldn't figure out if I was happy about the events that took place last night, or not.

I did close my eyes and try to fall back to sleep, but the events of last night flashed through me. I felt foolish for being one of those girls to sleep with someone on the first night of meeting them. I would've blamed the alcohol but this was all my own fault. I think I was just so excited to have finally found my mate, so happy to know that I wouldn't be mate less. The last few years had been so lonely that I couldn't stop myself from wanting a taste of that special companionship. I couldn't help but replay the scenes over in my head and shiver.

I looked back at clock to see that it'd been twenty minutes since the last time I had looked. I was too wired for the day to start, too anxious to see my handsome mate again. No matter how I felt about sex with Asher, I was still ecstatic to have found him. Today we would meet, talk and work everything out. I just hoped he wasn't one of those guys that felt intimidated by my bloodline. I didn't know his rank or what pack he was from but I prayed he wouldn't have any qualms about moving here.

Okay, it was time to get up. I couldn't ponder my thoughts anymore, I needed a distraction. As I sat up on the edge of the bed I felt my beast's restlessness and smiled. I looked out my window to see that the sun would be rising within the next hour. *I'll go for an early morning run.*

Hopefully being out in my other form would calm my beast a bit. I pulled a hoodie over my head as I headed to my bedroom door. I carefully snuck downstairs and out the front door of my house. I briskly walked towards the pack house, that already had rooms lit, not far from our home. Behind the pack house the trees slowly start to become thicker until you were swallowed up by the greenery.

When I was surrounded by the woods I pulled off my clothes making sure to knot my hoodie and shorts around my ankles. Seeing that my clothes are securely attached to my ankles I shifted. Every time I shifted I couldn't help but compare it to the night that I first shifted many years ago. The night would forever be burned into my brain because it was both the best and worst night of my life.

Until last night of course.

)) ● ● ● ● ((

I was sitting in the living room watching telly as mom played with my hair. Dad was still in his study working as we had just accepted new members into the pack. It had been a few weeks since my twelfth birthday and the awesome surprise party my parents had thrown me.

My father walked through the door into the living room to sit with mommy and me. My eyes starting to get droopy as I tried to watch the movie on the screen.

"Time for bed for you, Kira." Mother said as she moved me from her lap.

"No," I whispered. "NO…" I screamed as a wave on pain hit my body. I scrunched my eyes closed as my head started throbbing. I had similar pains before, mom and dad had said they were growing pains.

"Kira!" My mom said in her stern voice. I screamed, my skin felt too tight and hot. I heard my parents talking in the background as I tried not to focus on my body as it shook.

"She's about to shift." I heard my mother's voice cry. Immediately, I knew this pain wasn't any ordinary pain, I was going through my first shift. Weeks before my birthday my parents had sat me down and talked me through what would be happening soon. I was to go through my first shift and then I would be a full beast just like my mom and dad were.

My father picked me up and I opened my eyes slightly to see him carry me through the front door and outside into the cool quiet night.

24

LUNAR ACCORD

He laid me down on the ground as I let out my first howl. Tears streaming down my face as my first bone broke.

The age of a Lycans first shift depended on their family. The strong your family and the higher their title was the sooner you shifted to learn to protect those around you.

Going through your first shift was a big stage for us and caused for celebration within the family. It was a time to be loved and cherished, it was a very proud moment for parents and family members. First your body heated, your skin tightened then your bones start breaking one by one. Most Lycans and Weres alike, fell unconscious by the third or fourth break because it takes time to break each bone individually.

Once all your bones are broken, it then takes a few hours for your bones to grow and reshape themselves into the shape of a wolf.

By morning my first shift was completed and I was awoken by the sunlight. I looked around to see my parents in their Lycan forms sleeping around me.

))) ◉ ◉ ◉ (((

Shaking myself from my flashback, I took a minute to clear my mind and breathe in the fresh dawn air. I opened my eyes to see my big silver paws beneath me, holding me steady. My paws pounded the ground, crunching the forest floor as I ran.

When I was close to the northern border I started veering to the east already having a destination in mind; the lake in the middle of pack lands. I ran with all my might weaving in and out of the trees and leaping over bushes. I ran along the north-east border until I could see the pack gym and training center up ahead. I followed the path around the big building and into the woods opposite it.

It was another three miles or so until I neared the lake.

I dropped down onto my belly and crawled towards the water as the forest trees loomed above me. Relaxing and resting grew boring to my restless beast after a while. I rolled around in the fallen leaves and mossy ground. My eyes followed a family of birds as they flew amongst the trees chasing each other.

That's when I smelt something odd that I'd never scented before but it was oddly familiar. I followed the trail but keep quietly alert. I slowed my jog to a walk as I caught sight of the clearing smack bang in the middle of the eastern border.

It wasn't very big but it sure was beautiful in the spring when all the flowers were in bloom. And that's where I spotted him. Standing there, naked, in all his naked glory. I shifted and pulled on my hoodie and shorts that had been tied around my ankle.

"Asher?" I only paused to recognize that scent. It was him. And he was a rogue. I didn't know what to say, what to even think besides praying my beast would stop happily yipping around inside of me.

Rogues didn't mate with pack wolves. I couldn't believe that I hadn't caught his scent last night, I had mated with a rogue. He was my mate, an Alpha's mate… and he was a rogue Lycan! I must have had more to drink last night then I had originally thought. My heart was crushed as I wondered what was to happen now?

"I, Asher, leader to the rogues, reject this bond to Kira, Luna of Silver pack." My heart broke completely into a million pieces; I could do nothing but stare into those eyes. Those eyes that had held what I thought was loving sweetness only so few hours ago.

I knew what was to follow, over the next few days I

would be almost paralyzed with pain and sorrow. Over the next few weeks I would sink into a deep depression that I may or may not be able to come back out of. And finally, within the next few months I would finally shrivel up and die.

In our world, rejection of the mate bond wasn't an option. We were programmed as one half of a whole, put on this earth as pairs matched up by the Moon Goddess, Selene, herself. Unfortunately, there were stories of rejection written in the pack journals from many years ago.

Our main purpose, however shallow it may seem, was to find our mate and we couldn't live otherwise. But there was nothing else to be done, but to accept the inevitable. "I accept..." I couldn't look at him any longer, I paused and turned my head instead looking at a berry bush behind him. I released a low growl before continuing "I, *Alpha* of Silver pack, accept the rejection of Asher."

In this world respect is among the highest of mannerisms. A Luna is the Alpha males mate; an Alpha is of the Alpha bloodline and is born the next leader. I was an Alpha and having my bloodline challenged like that is greatly disrespectful.

I refused to call him by a title. Rogues were wolves who were either born as a rogue or had been banished from a pack. You didn't get kicked out of a pack for just anything, only unthinkable treason landed you as a rogue.

He was a filthy rogue, and nothing more. My beast may've been tied to him but even if he hadn't rejected me, I don't know what I would've done. I immediately shifted and ran back home.

I continued to run until I tired out, slowing to a jog until I finally collapsed on the ground. I looked around to see that I was near to the lake. Before long my family would know that I had mated and everyone else are soon to know that their future Alpha was mate less.

I was angry, so angry but at that moment my anger couldn't have surpassed the shock I was feeling. How? What…why? Why had the Moon Goddess cursed me so?

My eyes slowly closed with the heaviness of heartache and the shame of what I had done. Flames burned in my chest as I struggled. I felt it, the tearing of the mate bond within me. I awoke to a roaring headache and a snarling beast in front of me. Katherine, our Beta female, stood before me on all fours as a golden-brown Lycan wolf.

I lifted my head and opened the pack link to slowly let in all the chaos from my beloved pack. Katherine stepped closer and paused, lifting her muzzle in the air she sniffed and looked back at me.

Katherine and I walked back to my house in complete silence. As soon as my house came into view I saw my mother and father waiting on the front porch steps.

It was my mother who must have noticed my scent first, her eyes widened and her nose rose into the air slightly. Her eyes connected with mine first before turning to my father. My father sniffed the air and my eyes meet the ground to avoid his gaze as he must've realized it was my scent. When I peek my eyes up again my father has disappeared, my mother was talking to Katherine.

I slowly walked towards them, while I heard my mother speak. "Thank you for finding her and being so discreet Kathy."

"Of course Luna. I hope everything works itself out." My mother made a noise of agreement before Katherine bowed her head and left me standing just one meter before my mother. She held out my dressing gown and I shifted back quickly pulling it on. She reached for me with open arms and a tender expression. That was all it took to collapse into her with a burst of emotion.

My beast continued to whine inside of me but I couldn't do anything except block her out. My mind already being full enough with thoughts of my foolishness and stupidity as tears drowned my cheeks. I held tight to my mother as we crumbled to the steps of our front porch.

"Last night, at the party, I found my mate." I sobbed into in my mother's shoulder as I tried my hardest not to think his name. It hurt too much to think of him. Cutting the bond was like cutting a blood vessel, it was a part of who you are and was extremely painful.

"He's a rogue," As soon as I whispered out I heard a sharp gasp. "and he rejected me." I continued and my mother only pulled me tighter to her as she started to cry along with me. Not only had her daughter just gotten her heart broken but now she was also cursed to die. Lycan mates couldn't survive on their own.

As I made my way upstairs I could still hear my mother sobbing into my father on the couch downstairs. I felt guilty for causing them such heartache. I only told my mother what she needed to know, although I felt she'd have figured the rest out. In a way, I was glad to know that I wouldn't survive longer than a few months. I felt I wouldn't ever be able to let myself trust anyone ever again. If I had to live with this pain and heart break for the rest of my life it would be one miserable existence.

As I walked into my room, sat on my bed and saw that my alarm clock read just past noon. On my nightstand, next to my alarm clock my phone was flashing and buzzing with life. I picked it up to inspect the notifications; five missed calls and over a dozen texts. Opening the latest one, from Dante, it read;

If you're reading this, Carson and I went out looking for you. We hope you're safe. Please pick up your phone, we're worried as fuck! My mouth pulled into a small smile.

I put the phone on silent before replacing it back on the table. I'd have to remind myself later to text them back. I sat silently just staring at the dressing table mirror across from me. Along the edges of it were photos, notes and even some ticket stubs.

Looking to the center of the mirror it showed a version of myself I'd never seen before. The girl staring back at me had big hollow eyes. She was splashed with dirt and had pieces of the forest tangled in her hair. The shiver that ran down my spine was what kick started me to move.

I stepped into the shower to wash off that horrible night. It seemed that no matter how hard I scrubbed, I felt I'd never be clean again. Even my beast had disappeared on me, along with everything else I wasn't sure how I would survive the next month.

After the shower, I collapsed onto my bed and another wave of tears and pain flowed through me. That's where I stayed for two weeks; barely eating, not seeing anyone and not moving from my bed except when it was absolutely necessary. I knew my parents were worried sick but I didn't know how to help myself. All I wanted to do was wallow in the pain and self-pity that surrounded me.

At birth, your soul is entwined with someone else's, making you a part of each other. Whether you know it or not. With rejecting the bond, I had been tossed overboard in the middle of a storm, left on my own to drown. No matter how much deep breathing I did it didn't seem to calm the panic and pain filling my body, right down to my bones.

It was the fourteenth night of my own personal living hell when she came to me.

)))�𝕠𝕖𝕖(((

I was in the clearing on the eastern border, the one where my mate bond was forever broken. The only difference was all the flowers were in bloom making my surroundings shine in color.

At first sight I was alone but after a minute an angel appeared sitting on a garden bench. She was exactly how I imagined an angel to be. Dressed head to toe in a white flowy dress and the brightest white glow surround her.

"My child. Come, sit." Her soft melodic voice spoke gently and I couldn't help but walk to her.

"I am Selene and I am here to apologize for your pain." I intake a sharp breath, Selene the Moon Goddess herself. I kept thinking this must dream but I knew it wasn't, and that Selene must've really been here visiting me.

She let out a sigh as she looked at me, "I created Soul Mates so that my children would never be lonely. You were my only mistake. I'm sorry but all will be restored in time. I promise you, that you will survive all that has been put in your path."

"There is much more in store for you than you realize, Kira." She smiled softly at me.

"I don't understand." My eyebrows furrowed as I looked at her for more answers.

"I am afraid that I cannot say anymore. But I need you to promise me not to give up." She looked at me expectantly.

"Selene," I paused. "I promise, I'll do what you ask of me."

She wore a wide smile as she got up off the bench and looked around. "I must go, but I do hope to see great things from you."

I stood beside her, "Thank you." I bowed my head slightly in respect for our Goddess. She shimmered and disappeared, I sat back down to ponder what she said. I heard a flutter of wings from above and my head snapped towards the sound. The family of birds chasing each other.

CHAPTER THREE

As I WOKE UP I finally decided to pull myself together enough to go downstairs. I dressed in simple sweatpants and a t-shirt before I finally decided to walk down the stairs to the kitchen.

I hadn't left my room since that day. I had been in a depression coma for the past two weeks thinking of nothing but Asher. I knew through and through that it had been the right thing to do, to reject the bond. But, unfortunately, that didn't mean it hurt any less. I imagined if I had suddenly lost my sight, I'd have felt a similar way. Going all my life thinking about my mate and waiting for him to swoop in and sweep me off my feet, only for that rug to be ripped out from under me unexpectedly.

While it was still too soon to tell, I felt that the visit from the Moon Goddess might've done me some good. As of late, I'd barely found the motivation to eat and use the bathroom. The dream had me rattled but also began to bud a new sense of hope inside of me that everything would be okay.

My parents were sitting across from each other at the

dining room table when I entered the room. It was quiet, they were sat silently staring into each other's eyes. *Well, this wouldn't be awkward at all;* I rolled my eyes at my inner sarcastic bitch.

They had nearly fell out of their seats at the sight of me in the kitchen, up and out of bed. They fawned over me, rushing to make me my favorite breakfast. I felt pretty shitty for only being able to mutter a few words here and there. They had both been so supportive through all of this but I felt too vulnerable right now to let them see any deeper into the wound. I could barely look them in the eye, afraid to see the fear and pity that would be there.

After sitting and somewhat eating my breakfast with my parents, I made the decision that it was time to leave the house. Maybe the fresh air would do me some good. I hadn't wanted to see anyone lately, so my parents had been turning my friends away when they'd come to visit.

I knew I looked like shit because I felt it. My eyes and face were puffy, my skin took on a pasty pale color and from how loose my clothes felt; I'd definitely dropped a few pounds. Despite all that, I got dressed with as much effort as I could spare. It wasn't until I left the house that I started to notice the attitude changes in my pack mates. In a way, I wasn't surprised at the whisperings and looks, their future Alpha was mateless; meaning weak. After all, in a Lycans eyes a weak leader was an unwanted leader.

"I can't believe how much mess I've created," I cried into Dante's' shoulder shortly after arriving at her house. I hadn't meant to arrive a wreck but being in the outside hadn't agreed with me. The trees I saw made me think of Asher, mated couples on the street had made me dwell on the fact I would soon die alone, and the other pack members had only reminded me that I had failed them as their next leader.

"Half the pack's out hunting him, and the other half are just about planning an uprising against me." I paused to hiccup, "and the worst part about all of this, I'm all alone."

Dante went about to disagree but I waved her off, "I know that I have you and everyone else but I mean I'm mentally alone... the only thing that might've comforted me was knowing that I still had my beast." Dante gasped at the new information I was sharing, "She's gone, Dante."

Tears continued to pour down my face for a long while, it wasn't until they slowed down that she responded. "How long has it been?" She whispered.

"Since the rejection." My voice was ripped up from all the crying. We sat in silence with her hugging me close for I don't know how long. The first move was made by Dante as she looked up to the archway of her living room.

"The same thing happened with your aunt," Dante's mother, Allison, stood in the doorway with a sad expression on her face.

"What?" I asked, intrigued by what she'd said.

"Your Aunt Melissa." She released a sigh as she came over to sit with us.

"Melissa was a few years older than your mother but she and I were close friends."

"What happened? I only know that she died before I was born." I said confused as to why I hadn't heard anything about her before.

"She was eighteen when she met her mate. She was twenty-three when her mate went off to war and was killed." Her eyes started to get glassy as she reminisced about my aunt.

"Melissa was heart-broken. She lost her beast, pushed everyone away. After a while the pain had become too much for her to handle." My mother must've been worried that I'd have the same fate as my aunt. My more I thought on it the more weary I grew. My only hope was that the Moon Goddess was right.

After the past month, I finally felt bored. Bored and tired of being the poor shmuck of an Alpha who had gotten her heart broken. Although I had been gradually healing, my heart had still hurt, beating too fast in my chest every time I thought of him. Then I simply decided to just stop thinking of him, to stop torturing myself with questions of how he was coping or thoughts of his luscious hazel eyes. It wasn't like he deserved to have me thinking about him, like mom had said; he was unworthy of my thoughts.

That morning I'd woken with a new, and completely refreshed, energy flowing through my veins. Okay, so I didn't have a mate anymore, I had accepted that as my reality, still I felt lucky to be alive. My future would be a bit dimmer than originally thought out, that only meant I would have to try harder to fill it with joy and sunshine. I needed to throw myself back into life, and I thought pack training would be the perfect place to start.

What time is training today? I texted Carson as I jumped out of bed and pulled some leggings on. Before 'the incident' as I had taken to calling it, I had loved training. I was good at using my feelings to fuel my workouts and hone my skills. I hoped I hadn't completely lost my edge.

Do you really think training is wise? Her reply buzzed

through my phone quickly.

What time is training! I texted again completely ignoring her condescending text tone. The Moon Goddess said I would get past this, past him, so I needed to Alpha up. To start fighting for what I wanted, and the last few days I'd realized I wanted to live. I wanted so desperately to survive this pain. So today I would be doing just that. I was pushing the pain away, ignoring its existence.

The next few weeks after that, I fell into a very mundane routine. Every day I would train for hours with our Gamma, in human form, then I would hang out with Dante and Carson before heading home to spend time with my family. It was boringly normal, and I was loving every second of it. To just be back to a place where I could get out of bed in the morning and not feel like I was at risk of drowning.

It had been six weeks since the night I met that *Rogue*. It had been four weeks since I first left my bedroom after the rejection. Sadly, there was still no sign of my beast. She was still a presence inside of me, but it was like I was being denied access to her.

Cameron, the Gamma, was the person that trained me one on one, as our Deltas handled warrior and pack trainings.

Today, after training and washing up, I walked to Dante's for our trip to the local shopping mall. I hadn't ever been interested in shopping but I needed to buy a few things so Dante took that as a sign for a girl's day out.

Kira, I've sent Andrew to come keep an eye on you. My fathers' text vibrated through my phone. I internally groaned, I liked Andrew but my father had been paranoid as of late. Since not having my inner beast I had been reduced to hourly check-ins by my father and chaperoned play dates. Our Lycans were what made us different, they held all the power; without her I was basically just a simple human. It was seriously frustrating to be treated like a toddler while in your twenties.

"Well, hello to you too grumpy Gus!" I looked up to see Dante holding her front door wide open.

"Sorry, dad just texted that Andrew will be joining us."

"As expected." Dante nodded along in agreement with my father, I annoyingly was not going to get any sympathy about this matter from her.

"Don't look so happy to see me, Kira." Andrew chuckled as he wrapped his arm around my shoulder, smiling as always, his presence coming seemingly out of nowhere and startling me.

My human abilities had weakened significantly since losing my beast; so, I had been on edge. Without having my beast my heightened hearing, sight and sense of smell had all gone downhill. Even my healing ability had gone kaput, I bumped into a door frame the other day banging my elbow. I was still marred with the bruise.

"I've been so bored. Tyler has been working so much lately, some days not even coming home." Carson droned on as Dante dragged me into yet another clothes store.

I hadn't seen too much of Carson lately. I had tried really hard to avoid lovey-dovey mated couples. It's not their fault and I was truly happy for Carson and Tyler but there was only so much mushy crap I could handle while also dealing with fact that I'd be alone for the rest of my life, however long that may actually be.

However, I still loved Carson as though she was a sister

and today I was very happy to be spending time with both her and Dante. Despite my lack of love for shopping, we'd had a good time but then came the dreaded part; unloading the bags into the house. While the others had mainly just bought clothes, I bought things to keep me and my mind occupied. Books, CDs, movies, some games, even a jigsaw puzzle.

Mum, dad and I were seated around the coffee table in the living room playing a game of the newest monopoly version when Delta John burst through the front door with Kyle and Tyler in his wake.

"Alpha. We've found them." He said as he puffed out a breath of air.

John was one of our three Deltas. A Delta was a high ranked pack warrior that dealt with trainings and tracking missions. Along with Kyle and Tyler, John was chosen as a Delta because he was very skilled. A Silver pack practice was that we chose our Deltas based on their keen senses and abilities not on their lineage.

Dad stood up from the couch, the board game we were all playing totally forgotten. As the Deltas followed my father into his study I couldn't help my interest being peaked. My head shifted to look at my mother. I squinted my eyes at her wondering what the hell was going on.

"Kira Leigh Brookes! If you keep staring at me, you'll burn a hole through my head. Is that what you want? To behead your own mother?" She gave me that look, that eyebrows raised scolding look reserved for a mothers' use only. Not my first time being on the receiving end of it but one of the only few times I ignored it.

"Mother, what's going on?" There must've been something big going on for all three of them to barge in like that. Truth be told I was surprised and upset that my father hadn't tagged me in to what was going on.

She sighed, giving in to my pleading look, "They've been out scouting for your mate."

She hadn't even finished her sentence before I was up and bursting through my father's office doors.

"You found him?" I wasn't sure what I was feeling or what was happening but I knew that I should've definitely been in that room if they were discussing anything that had to do with *my* bastard mate.

I realized at that moment that he wasn't my mate but my ex-mate. That thought stung for a second before adding more fuel to my fire. We were rejected Lycan mates, once you broke that bond, that link between you, there was no turning back. We would never be mates again. That's why rejection among Lycans was so rare. You got only one shot to be truly happy, and I threw mine out the window without a second thought. And I knew I had done the right thing too.

Other species were different. I knew that werewolves could go back and forth between their mates all they liked. They could even choose to mate with someone else, they called it a choice mate. Ha. I laughed cynically at that thought, stupid spoilt werewolves that they were. I supposed that was one of the reasons we were the superior species, not having your true mate by your side made you, especially an Alpha, weak.

Pulling back to reality as my dad stood up and spoke, "Kira! You shouldn't be in here; you don't need to be included in any of this." I glanced around at everyone in the room, all of my father's council were there; our Beta, Gamma, and his Deltas. I was this packs next Alpha I was to be privy to all going-ons in my pack.

My eyebrows scrunched, *when had Noah and Cameron gotten here?*

"I want to be here; I need to know what's going on if it's something serious." I walked to the only place to sit in my father's packed office, the window seat. I remembered as a child I used to like to sit there and read because of the atmosphere that the beautifully full bookshelves and afternoon sunshine had provided.

My father had spoken of revenge on my mate for what he did to me. I even knew that he was out searching for him with warriors, but never in my wildest dreams did I think that he would have found him. I figured *he* wouldn't have been anywhere close to this pack, otherwise I would have met him a long time ago.

Over the past few weeks I had tried to block everything out. Even after I started going out, I ignored all that was going on around me. I had heard the doubts and whispers as soon as I first left the house weeks ago now.

'I wonder what's wrong with her, no one ever gets rejected'

'Her mate doesn't want her, why should we?'

'She has no control over her mate bond, how does she expect to have control over a whole pack'

I had started to believe them; I would make a terrible Alpha. *You don't have time for a pity party right now.* I scolded myself as my thoughts had started to dangerously drift.

"We finally found how he got through the border patrol and we followed his tracks from there," John stood as he spoke.

"He was with other rogues; they had set up camp past the Crescent Moon and Blue Wolves territories. We don't know how long they've been there or why he even came here in the first place. Scouting for information maybe?" Kyle informed the rest of us.

'They're building an army.'

It was the softest of whispers but it wasn't me who had thought it. The accusation came from deep within me leading me to believe it was my Lycan. She hadn't spoken or made an appearance in weeks, I was shocked. I had thought that I'd never see or hear from my beast again.

It had made sense, what she said, he was probably here scouting for weak points or even for new recruits.

"'Leader to the rouges…'" Everyone's heads whipped to me and I realized I must have pondered that out loud. I cleared my throat. Telling everyone, no matter how much I trusted them, details of my rejection was going to be like getting my belly button piercing torn out.

"I, Asher leader to the rogues…" I decided to end there as their faces started showing powerful signs of pity. I almost rolled my eyes at the big, scary men of our pack turning gooey on me.

"He had said 'leader to the rogues.' That must mean he's leading some sort of army." There were sharp intakes of breath and murmuring as soon as I had spoken. I couldn't believe that over the last six weeks I hadn't given this any thought at all. That asshole was actually building an army? What the fuck, who even did that anymore? I felt like such an idiot as I stood looking around at the men that crowded the room.

"Alpha, there's something else. We're afraid that he may have caught us. We had become sloppy with all our attempts at finding them that we may have left a scent behind. If anyone picks it up, they're going to be led straight here." Kyle adds in while looking down ashamed and submitting to my father.

"Hmm." My father sitting in his office chair behind the desk thinks on his Deltas mistake.

"We shall double patrols and ready everyone for battle; mandatory trainings, no one leaves the territory and a curfew shall be set for all pack wolves." As they began strategizing, I snuck out and up to my room. My back flopped to my bed as I needed to think.

The main thought in my mind was a surprise, quite comical in a way, but also angering. *That rat bastard rogue took my virginity. No, I let that rat bastard take my virginity.*

And now he was building an army and most likely leading that army to war, against my pack. I'd love to have thought that the war was over me; maybe two males were fighting over me or maybe I was being held hostage and my hero was coming to my rescue. Not even fucking close. The betrayal that ebbed inside of me was enough to cause a lone tear to streak from the corner of my eye.

I was upset, angry and hurt all at the same time. Not mentioning the feelings of betrayal and guilt, my emotional state was an absolute shipwreck. I sighed out and fell into a very long night's sleep.

CHAPTER FOUR

THE SUN WAS JUST STARTING to leak into my room when my mother barged in to wake me.

"Honey! Kira, wake up dear." I heard my mother's voice rush around my bedroom. As I blinked my eyes open, suddenly light filled my vision and burned my eyes. I slowly sat up, my eyes adjusting to the light, to see my mother fussing.

"Kira. It's happening. The war we've been anticipating is here."

"What?" I yelled.

"The rogues we've been hunting, we've found them. Unfortunately, they've arrived here sooner than we expected..." She started to mumble off towards the end. We heard the howl from outside telling us this was it, shit's about to go down. I heard, in the distance, an explosion and instantly hoped no one was close to it.

My mother looked in to my eyes as she whispered, "Your mate is here." I couldn't contain the gasp that sounded from my lips. Since that meeting yesterday I had the strangest feeling, like something was wrong. Now it proved my instincts had been right. I felt immense guilt for the fact that he was my mate while he was coming to attack my family.

Looking up from my bed I saw my mother filling a backpack with items from around my room.

"Mother! What are you doing? I'm not leaving." I stood firm as I caught on to what exactly she was packing for. It was in my nature to fight and protect. No matter how much over the last month I've wanted to just disappear I wouldn't leave at a time like this. I couldn't, this was my pack. Whether they liked me or not these were my people, my friends and my family.

"Just in case, Kira." She whispered as she conceded to my commanding Alpha tone.

Another bomb went off but this one was a lot closer to the house as I felt the slight shake underneath my feet. I quickly changed my clothes, putting my dagger in its sheath tied to my waist. Deeply hidden inside my closet I pulled out my sword that I kept for protection.

Since I've had no wolf, Cameron had been working extra hard on my other capabilities, such as slicing a Lycans head clean off with a sword. It had proved to be something I was good at and very much enjoyed. With me suited up we hurried downstairs and my mother immediately started to escort what women and children she could into the bunker below our house.

"Your father and I love you very much Kira, if any happens always remember that. I'm so proud to have such a beautiful strong Alpha for a daughter." She said, pausing what she was doing to give me a bone crushing hug. A tear slipped out of my eye as I prayed to the moon that this was not the last time I ever saw her.

LUNAR ACCORD

"I love you mom."

"Kira, you aren't a Lycan anymore, please be careful."
She gave me a pleading look as I rushed to the front door.
Worriedly leaving my mother behind, I hurried out to the
field where I saw wolfish beasts everywhere.

The fight was already in motion, I paused to suck in a
big breath. Immediately I regretted it because of all the foul
odors inhibiting our pack lands. *Filthy rogues needed a damn
bath!*

This wasn't a drill. I opened my eyes to see a light brown
Lycan wolf lunge at me, its jaw snapping at my neck.
Grabbing my pocket knife, I slid under him and sliced his
belly open. He collapsed instantly and I turned to my next
target. I had never killed anyone before but now was not
the time to think twice on the subject.

I heard the continuing of bombs going off, my guess
was the landmines nearer to the border had been activated.
I quickly scanned the area looking for my friends, knowing
that Carson and Tyler were out here. As I killed off my
third rogue wolf, I spotted Carson a hundred yards or so
off to my right. I ran toward her, stabbing and slicing what
Lycans I could on the way. I moved back-to-tail with
Carson to cover her from behind as she fought off two
small mud colored rogues.

I lunged for a silver wolf coming towards me, dicing
into her front leg with my sword. As she tried yanking away
from me her teeth pierced my arm, yanking it roughly. I
gradually felt the pain intensify until finally I heard a crack.
I screamed out at the pain, her jaw dislodged from my arm
as she was thrown from me. The wound quickly started
leaking blood. I stared into her blood red eyes snarling as
Jasper, a pack warrior, barreled into her side then quickly

snapped her neck before moving on.

I looked around the clearing as the ground vibrated softly beneath me, I saw wolves still left fighting but also countless lifeless bodies lying around. I noticed the explosions had gradually slowed down.

I spotted my father to see him sparring with Asher. I gulped down while nodding to Carson, I jogged over avoiding the last few fighting wolves. I tried not to move my arm as it burned with an uncomfortable heat.

I didn't know what I'd do when I got to my father but I knew that I needed to aid him. After all, I had caused all of this. I was nearly there when I saw my father get struck down. My eyes hardened and I ran as fast as I could. Facing my mate, he gave me a wolfy grin and that only made me even more furious.

Wielding my sword, we started to circle each other and I immediately tried to pinpoint his weak spots. He didn't seem to have any but I did notice his tell. His wolf wasn't overly big in size and I started to feel hope rise in my chest.

He made the first move towards me growling out, he leaped forward trying to scare me. If I hadn't been on such an adrenaline high, it might've. At this point in time I was only a human girl holding a sword facing a wolf. I dodged his next attack and slipped behind him. I sliced my dagger straight through his tail making him snarl at me and whip around. I heard a low growl from my left and saw another rogue. I panicked for a split second before he ran off into the forest.

Asher made one last attempt to disarm me by rising onto his hind legs. His giant paws flew around until he caught me. His claw caught the side of my face. I groaned at the pain as I backed away and tried to reboot, lucky that

I had turned slightly at the last second. My sword clattered to the ground as he knocked me down.

We struggled on the ground as I felt warm liquid trail down the side of my face and into my hair. I flung my dagger around with my good arm, trying to sink into anything I could. The next thing I heard was a very loud growl, I looked to see it coming from Noah. Asher snarled out backing up, he paused to look me straight in eye. I hobbled to a standing position as carefully as I could, holding my arm, careful not to move it.

You could only tell a rogue from a pack wolf from their eyes. Rogue eyes were tinted red to tell them apart, to warn packs that they were a wild savage beast.

I felt saddened as I was considering my mates' eyes. They held no ounce of pain or regret, those eyes were telling me that he wasn't finished ruining my life just yet. He turned and bounded off into the woods, smart enough to know that he would not have beaten the both of us. Coward that he was.

I looked over to Noah, nodded my head in thanks and he nodded back. I saw the leftover rogues starting to pull back knowing this fight wouldn't be one that either of us would win. Only once I had seen that my pack was safe did I run to my father's side. He hadn't moved, "Dad! Please daddy, please wake up." I shook him trying to wake him.

I checked for a pulse but came up with nothing. Tears streamed down my face as a medic came over to see to him. After the CPR doesn't work she looked up to me and silently shook her head.

I looked down and just let it all out. I felt like I was trapped under this crushing weight that wouldn't budge.

The pressure in my chest only got worse as I thought of my mother, how would she live without my father. The medic finished cleaning and stitching the gash that stretched all the way down the side of my face. For a quick moment, I felt lucky that the gash wasn't an inch over otherwise it would've caught my eye.

"This will heal without a problem; the stitches are dissolvable so as long as you don't pull at them you'll be fine." She inspected my arm and shoulder next before coming to her conclusions. She popped my arm back into its socket and then wrapped a sling around my forearm to my neck.

"I suspect it's fractured. There's not much that can be done at the moment, I'm afraid." I looked to the medic who had come over to see to my wounds and asked about the Luna, my mother. *Was she alright? Where was she?*

The medic backed away and looked down, she pointed over to the middle of the field. I looked, squinting to spot my mother, my eyes trying not the linger on all the injured pack members and those lying lifeless on the ground. Then I realized my mother wasn't stood helping our pack but on the ground with blood pouring from her mouth.

I slowly advanced to her as medics started covering all our dead with white sheets. As I walked to her I saw the medic start to cover her with a similar sheet. I paused at her body and stopped the medic from covering her face. I sunk to the ground and rested my mother in my lap.

Stroking her hair, the tears continued to stream down my cheeks. In a matter of hours my whole world had come crashing down around me. *Wasn't it bad enough that he had rejected me, he had to come in and take everything else from me too.*

My heart broke as I sat looking around the pack. So

many people lost their mates, their mothers, daughters, brothers and fathers. Guilt ate away at me, my mate had caused all of this. I feared I would never be free of a guilty conscience or my heart empty of sorrow. I vowed at that very moment to make sure he was sent down to the depths of hell for all he'd done. I tried my hardest to pull myself together as I looked around to analyze the damage. I blew out a long breath as I saw my pack mates starting to look around, wondering.

"What will we do now?" I heard as families huddled around our fallen Lycans. In that moment it would've been so easy to slink back, let someone else deal with the mess I'd indirectly created.

I looked to Noah, he gave me a nod of encouragement, something I really needed. I had really and truly lost my everything, I only found the will to continue as I looked around into the lost eyes of our pack. They needed me to guide them. I pushed my own thoughts and feelings to the deepest, darkest pits of my mind. I genuinely hoped to lose them forever, but I knew I wouldn't be that lucky.

"We will seek refuge in the Shadow Pack." I said as I find my voice after catching the crowds eye. It was the only solution I could think of. The Shadow pack was my aunt and uncles pack and I knew they would gladly take us in. As for our land, I wasn't sure what would happen to it. Maybe I could've lent it out to a neighboring pack. The Crescent Moon pack were quite big already but I knew they were always expanding their pack numbers.

"Move the bodies to a pile to be burned." I instructed trying to keep my voice from wavering. As I looked around at all the devastation surrounding me I tried my hardest to remember what the moon goddess had said to me all those weeks ago.

'You will survive all that has been put in your path.' She had promised. Did she mean this? Did she know that this would happen? *Of course she did.* And, although I was confused as to why she hadn't warned me I also knew that I had to trust her wise words.

As pack members placed their loved ones on the big fire pit Noah started speaking of our fallen pack mates. I stood in the back of the crowd until our Alpha and Luna were placed on the fire last. I moved my way through the crowd and to Noah's side.

Everyone, including myself bowed our heads at the loss of our beloved leaders; my ever-cherished parents. After a moment of silence people starting quietly chatting amongst themselves.

"Everyone, prepare yourselves for a journey. Eat, rest and mourn now for we need to leave as soon as possible. We'll leave within an hour." I commanded. I knew it was unlikely for the rogue Lycans to come back so soon after an attack but I didn't want to risk it. The sooner we left the better. And so, that's what happened; pack members ate, rested and mourned while myself, Noah and my council prepared for our travels.

I helped as much as I could, wanting to get as far away from here as possible before it got dark. Right now, it was about eleven am, by noon we would be on our way to our new home. I calculated that it would've taken me three days to get to my Aunts by running in my beasts' form. With injured pack mates, including women and children it could take anytime between five and eight days.

I quickly searched for Dante and her family rushing over to make sure they were okay. Dante's' Father had a cut on his arm but it had been stitched and they weren't worried about it.

I left Dante with a tight hug as I spotted Carson in the distance with Tyler and their families. While I made my way over to them I checked in with a few other pack members on the way. One girl, Sammy, had lost her mother in the fight and was clutching onto her father and her younger brother.

I also stopped to tend to a pair of women that had been my mothers' close friends. They had said they were okay just a bit shaken, saddened by the pack members that were lost. Of course, they also gave me their deepest condolences saying that the fallen Alpha and Luna would be terribly missed.

Before setting off I emptied my father's safe, I had my own bank account but I wasn't sure if I'd ever come back to this place. I took a register of our current pack members and our recently deceased pack members to give to my uncle for his records. Our pack wasn't ever big and we weren't very well known, we had just less than sixty people in our pack. Now we had about thirty.

That night when we stopped for food and rest was the first real chance I had to think to myself. I could only hold in my pain because as I looked around at my pack members I saw more than enough pain there, I didn't want to add to it.

His eyes haunted me as I took the first shift on look out. The forest was dark and quiet, I had nothing to distract myself with except my thoughts. Thoughts of him.

Had he really not felt anything for me? For the breaking of our mate bond? It hurt to think that but I was also slightly jealous. Why should I be the one to feel all the pain? I hadn't even done anything wrong.

His eyes appeared in the darkness of the forest and I tried to scream but my voice came out silent, as if I hadn't spoke at all. I looked around in panic, wilding searching for someone, for anyone as his beast stepped out of the shadows and closer to me.

I was terrified and shaking, I was trapped. The shaking began faster and I faintly heard my name. My eyes darted everywhere looking for the voice but I could find anything.

"Kira." I knew that voice.

"Kira, wake up." I shook as I was pulled from the dark forest, from my tormentor. My eyes fluttered open to see Andrew and Katherine standing in the morning light.

I huffed a sigh of relief as my eyes fluttered around focusing on all my pack members around me. It was just a dream, thank the Goddess for some mercies.

"We're waking everyone up and getting prepared to leave." Katherine spoke softly to me as she and Andrew left me to wake the other pack members.

I munched on a granola bar as I finally wandered over to where Noah was standing with the Deltas. Carson had been fine aside from a few odd cuts and scrapes. Tyler on the other hand had lost his older brother and his family were smothered by the grief. I gave my deepest sympathy before moving on.

"Good morning Alpha," Noah said and the others followed his lead bowing their heads in respect.

As Noah dismissed the ranks he turned to me, "I fell asleep on guard last night," I said.

"I know," he chuckled. "Don't worry I covered the rest of your shift." I looked up at him and smiled my thanks.

As we continued talking we decided that since we would shortly be in new territories I would run ahead with

Gamma Cam and Delta Tyler to speak to different Alphas about crossing their pack lands and resting on their borders. I was sure that the Alphas' wouldn't pose an issue seeing our circumstances but I was determined to protect what was left of our pack.

))◐◉●◐◖◖(

I didn't know where the hell we were but I knew we had been travelling for nearly six days now, we had only been stopping and resting when absolutely necessary.

The first couple of days the gash on the side of my face had still been leaking a bit but I managed to change the bandages whenever I could. The bandage currently on was mainly just to keep it from getting infected. We weren't exactly in a clean environment. My arm was harder to deal with because there wasn't anything I could do for it except keep movement to a minimum.

We had passed through five different pack territories on our journey so far and the rest had been human lands. While the few uninjured warriors and Deltas may have been handling our travels okay, most others weren't. On top of having women and children with us, most warriors or higher ranked had injuries.

From what Kyle and John had detected we had just passed the New Hampshire state border, and were currently on pack lands. I slowed down at the front of the pack to a walk and waited for everyone to gather. Only the ranked in our pack knew that I couldn't reach my inner beast or shift. That wasn't information that I wanted our pack to know, especially not now in such a state of dismay.

I volunteered to lead the pack hoping to hide my weaknesses from them. I was too stubborn to show the effects losing my parents had on my mental state, too proud to let the physical pain leak through the cracks. I felt my people didn't need to know how much agony their Alpha was really in, it would only lead to more pessimism. Once we came to a more permanent stop, that would be my time to cry and collapse. I only had to hold myself, the crumbling mountain, together long enough to arrive at my Aunt and Uncle's.

"Everyone, shift back and rest up here. We'll run up ahead and scout for any locals."

"Ten minutes," I ordered as turned to Cam and Tyler, letting them catch their breath and grab a drink before we started scouting ahead. Over the past few days I had panicked a few times not knowing exactly whose territory and which pack we were crossing.

I had trained all my life to know the packs and the pack leaders that covered the country, I had even visited and met a few. But I had to say it was completely different learning them to travelling through them. Lucky for me, Noah and the other ranked wolves were there to help and guide as much as they could.

From what I remembered, the closest pack would be the Night pack but I didn't know where their territory borders were. If the Night pack were close by than I was more than a little nervous. They were a large and highly trained pack, making them extremely dangerous.

I had heard even worse things about their Alpha. I had never liked gossip but when you didn't know the truth sometimes rumors were the only thing you had to go on.

It was said that Alpha Caius was cursed, I heard that he didn't have a mate. Of course, I had also heard that he had kidnapped, locked away and killed his mate but I definitely thought that was a bit extreme. There must be some sort of explanation or story as to why he was 'cursed.'

In a way, I could empathize, I didn't have a mate and I had heard what some of the people in my pack had said about me. I didn't even want to imagine what lies would be spread about me outside of my pack.

"Noah," I called his attention briefly away from his mate. "Keep an eye out, we still don't know who's lands we're on."

He nodded and I gathered with Cam and Tyler. Most minor injuries of our pack members had healed which is why I felt okay in climbing on Cams back after he had shifted. *A privilege that came with being a Lycan. Which I was currently not.*

Cam and Tyler ran side by side as fast as they could, in their beast forms, inland while I tried my hardest not to cause any more discomfort to my arm. We travelled through the trees for about half an hour before we caught another Lycans scent. We started to follow the scent but it was only a few minutes later that they both pulled to a halt.

It wasn't long until I heard the pounding of footsteps following ours.

"Swerve to the left." I yelled to them swerving around a tree and over to the left though it wouldn't surprise whoever was following as they probably would've heard me.

I knew it was pointless to continue running as I saw wolves ran up alongside us. Low growls filled the air as even more Lycans appeared up ahead. My head whipped around wildly to see that we were surrounded even as we ran.

Not that it would make much difference but at least we would all try to defend our pack together. The pack closed in on us but there was way too many to fight off with just the three of us. That didn't mean we wouldn't try our damn hardest though.

We stood back to back as we searched for a gap, our way out. A dark brown wolf stepped forward towards us. My eyes zeroed in on him wishing I could growl along with my pack mates. He seemed to radiate some power but not nearly enough to be an Alpha. He still took offence at my Gamma and Delta's growling.

He stepped closer and closer, I glared even harder the closer he got. He shifted to his human form in front of us making me look away out of instinct but quickly look back to keep my eyes on the target.

"You're trespassing." He spoke to me seeing as I was the only one in human form but I completely ignored him. "Shift." His command went out to Cameron and Tyler.

When he was about a meter away I lunged forward disregarding the sling from around my neck. All hell broke loose around me but I focused on the threat in front of me. As I attacked him other wolves started wailing on me but I didn't give up. Giving up is like admitting defeat, and I wouldn't willingly be defeated.

More and more wolves appeared around me clouding my vision, I punched and kicked at everything while also trying to clamp my teeth through anything I could. I knew that I was only creating more pain for my body to deal with later but in that moment, I didn't care.

I didn't last long before I saw the leaders' brown wolf again, he barreled me into a tree where my head slammed hard against its thick trunk. I tried to blink but everything was hazy and I knew I'd lost this fight.

CHAPTER FIVE

MY HEAD WAS POUNDING AND that seemed to be what woke me up. I softly blinked my eyes open and was thankful that there wasn't much light. I slowly rolled over onto my back trying to look around for anything familiar about this place. It's only when I really took notice of my surroundings that I knew where I was.

I shot up but groaned in pain clutching my side. The pain spread throughout my body and I couldn't determine where the origin of it was. *I was in a prison cell!*

Within the cell was a cot I was currently sitting on and a tiny porthole window high on the back wall. I turned to see there were two concrete walls on either side of me and a cell wall made of silver laced bars. Lycans and werewolves alike are both burned by silver which is why it being used in prison buildings was not uncommon.

I creeped to the front of the cell, peaking out to see that there was a row of many cells on each side of the darkly lit corridor. I looked to the cell across from me but I could only make out two cots opposite from each other.

I huffed out and sunk down to the cold concrete floor.

How long had we been here? Was it hours? Days? I wasn't sure. I looked along to the other cells and can't help but blame myself that my people were in here. I inspected the framing of the silver barred door. No way would I be able to escape, I wouldn't even be able to touch it without being injured.

As I sniffed around I saw a tray in the corner of the room, I slid closer to try and get a better look. Instantly I shoved away from it and back to the cot as I smelt the horrendousness of what food was on that tray, how long had it been there? Surely it wasn't put in fresh for me.

That's when I finally took notice of the cast on my arm. Why would they waste a doctors' time on me if they were only going to throw me in a cell anyway? I quickly lifted my hand to my face, feeling the bandage was still in place. That was a small relief.

Through the porthole, I saw above ground that it was late at night and most likely everyone was asleep and wouldn't be waking up for some time. I decided I may as well try to get some more rest as there wasn't anything for me to do until sun up.

It must have been hours that I was sat staring at that porthole waiting for the sun to rise. My body must have had all the rest it could've wanted because my eyes were determined to stay wide open and alert. My mind took over with thoughts of my parents and replaying their last moments. It was the first time I'd gotten a quiet moment to myself.

The sunlight was peeking in through the small window when I heard my pack members start to awaken. In the light, I spied two guards at the end of hallway but I needed to capture their attention.

"HEY! I need some help here!" I screamed out at the top of my lungs. I looked to see they hadn't even turned my way, only continuing to talk to each other. I took a deep breath before trying to tap into my Alpha command. I wasn't sure how well it would work because my Lycan hadn't been present in a while, and these wolves were loyal to another Alpha.

"COME HERE." I commanded. I pulled myself back to try and collect myself. That took a lot of effort but I noticed that it had worked in my favor. I heard the footsteps and stood up a little straighter which only resulted in me doubling over with the pain of my side.

I heard the thundering footsteps stop at my cell but I couldn't stand straight. I sunk to my butt clutching my side and looked up at the guard. He was stocky and was probably about the same age my dad had been. He had dark hazel eyes and dark slightly long hair.

"I demand to speak to someone." This guy may have scared a regular wolf with his size and his obvious experience but definitely not me or my Alpha genes.

"You are speaking to someone." He sassed me with a roll of his eyes.

"I meant, someone important around here." My mouth twisted into a slight smirk at my insulting him.

"Cregg!" The other guard called out in warning to the guy, Cregg.

"Where is your Alpha?" I demanded to know with a narrowed gaze.

"He's busy. He'll come when he's not busy." He said gruffly and walked away.

"Tell him the Alpha of Silver pack is waiting to speak

with him." I groaned, exasperated at seeing that there was nothing more to do but wait.

I looked to the cell across from me and saw two people. *It was so very rude and inconsiderate that I didn't get a roommate.* As I looked closer I could make out the features of Tyler and Carson. Without thinking I ran to the cell door wanting to be closer to my friends, happy that they were safe. My hands singed as they came into contact with the silver barred door, I stumbled back at the pain of the burns. I heard laughter from the guards as I yelped out at the contact. *I'm such an idiot.*

"Kira! Are you okay?" Carson said as her and Tyler moved as close to the cell bars as possible without making my mistake.

"Yeah, just stings." I groaned out but tried my best to smile.

"How long have we been here? How long was I out for?" I asked getting straight to the point while trying my best to ignore the immense burning in my hands.

"We were dragged here two and a half days ago, Alpha." Tyler answered me with his tone that meant business. I nodded to him and started to think on what he said.

Two and a half days I had been out and my wounds still hadn't healed. I made a mental note to try and hide my injuries as much as possible. My pack could not know that I wasn't presently linked to my beast.

"Has anything happened while I was out other than being brought here?"

"No. Everyone seems to have been mostly unharmed and those who were harmed are healing. The Alpha hasn't come yet, no one but the guards have been here." I sighed out in relief at hearing my pack was relatively okay.

"When did I get this?" I lifted my arm to point it out.

"We were here before you, that must have been why she came in later." She said turning to speak more directly to Tyler.

I awoke again but this time it was to the thundering slam of a door. I was instantly alert and looking through the bars. I saw the brown wolfed moron from the forest walking down the steps behind the guards' station.

"Bring her to Inter 3." He spoke to them but I strained my ears to take in every word he said. He turned and walked through a door beside the stairs as the guards started walking. They again stopped at my cell, the one that wasn't Cregg pulled out the key to open my door.

"You have been summoned." Cregg said to which my face twitched trying to control my burning anger. I took a long breath as I walked out the open door. They will not need to drag me anywhere, I'd go willingly. If to only say what I had to say to whoever was in charge.

The other one clasped my hands loosely behind my back and walked me forward to the door the moron went through. As I walked down the corridor I sensed my pack mates looking at me and I held my head a little higher.

On the other side of the door I saw another small corridor with thick steel doors on each side, five in total. We stopped part way down the hall and turned to a door. It was a small and cringy room that they shoved me into. There was a lightbulb hanging in the center of the room over a metal chair and that was all.

As he lightly shoved me towards the chair I got a better look at the inside walls. I shivered at the sight of silver chains and cuffs attached to the side wall. Everything may have looked clean but I knew what went on in interrogations. The room may as well have been painted with blood from the strong smell of bleach.

I was an Alpha, it was my job to lead interrogations not to be interrogated, this felt weird; against nature. I just hoped I didn't piss anyone off while I was here. If I explained clearly they should let us all free, and it made me feel better that we had proof of our journey.

I shrunk down into the large metal chair letting its coldness cradle me as I tried to calm myself. Having landed not only myself, but my entire pack, in prison cells did nothing to my already doubted abilities as a leader.

As the door wrenched open it showed a man that may or may not have been the man I attacked back in the forest. *And shit, I was doomed.*

He cleared his throat as his eyes narrowed, shooting imaginary arrows at my head. He was actually quite cute, now that he was fully clothed and I could take a proper look at him. Tall, well built, spiked dark brown hair. He straightened standing in the doorway and stepped forward towards the corner of the room.

My eyes were solely trained on his every movement that they completely missed who had replaced his spot in the doorway. *Oh, my Moon Goddess.*

Standing tall with power radiating off him at a hundred miles an hour, he was the Alpha. If I hadn't been an Alpha myself I would've been terrified that I had looked into the eyes of such a strong Lycan leader. I tried to keep my expression neutral but again, he was blindingly handsome.

He walked to stand in front of me then paused looking back at the door as it closed. His hair was short at the sides but longer on top, the color resembling that of a raven's feathers. I realized maybe he was waiting for me to speak first, I had been the one to call for him. A small blush colored my cheeks with embarrassment.

"My name is Kira Brookes, Alpha of the Silver pack."

Mr. hotness in front of me bent to his knees in front of me, squinting while his eyes were flitting across my features.

"It's nice to meet you…" I had had an idea of who he was and where we were but I wasn't prepared to make an idiot of myself if I was wrong.

I didn't hold any hatred or ill will towards him or his pack. I just wished they had of waited a second to hear our explanation before capturing us and locking us away. Then again, I suppose I did attack that moron from the forest first.

"Caius Matthews, Alpha of the Night pack." My suspicions were confirmed and I gave a polite smile. I looked to the corner of the room gesturing to the other guy. His only response was to scoff and look away.

"Trenton Grand. Beta of the Night pack." I turned to look back at the Alpha when he was the one to respond. Well I wasn't asking much, just his name and he wouldn't even answer. Wow, he must really hate me if he's getting his Alpha to answer my questions on his behalf. After sending Trenton a small glare to show I did not appreciate his attitude, I turned back to the Alpha.

"Now, why don't you tell me what you're doing on my lands?" Said the Alpha with a teasing smirk on his face.

"Ten days ago, Silver pack lands were attacked," I paused rethinking how much I should be telling him, I'll stick to the basics.

"Many casualties and many injured." A small sigh leaves my body at the thought of all the pack members we lost in battle, my parents top of that list. I looked up making sure they were listening before I continued, which they were. Their brows were furrowed, they must not have heard about the attack yet.

"We're on our way to the Shadow pack. Alpha Liam and Luna Mary are expecting us; we will seek permanent refuge with them."

"I, along with my Gamma and Delta, were on our way to meet with you as we were captured. We were coming to seek permission to rest on your borders before continuing on our way. I swear upon our pack members grave that we are no threat." It was silent as I looked at the Alpha, almost pleading him to believe me and to let us continue on our way.

"I shall check out your story before I let you and your pack free. You will wait here where an eye can be kept on you." With that he stood to his full height and walked out the door, his Beta following right behind. He was only looking out for his pack and it was in their best interests to watch us closely until they knew we could be trusted.

It must have been hours of sitting staring at the concrete walls, at the chains hanging in front of me and at the door, praying that it would open. My eyes started to flutter closed and I could feel sleep pulling me into its depths and away from my undying boredom; I was thankful.

Ripped away from sleep by a clang, I sat alert, my eyes scanning for the source of a potential threat. When I saw that it was only Alpha Caius I relaxed. Seconds later, perking up knowing that this meant we were free to finally leave.

"You and your park are free to go." My heart sagged in relief at the thought of regaining my packs freedom.

"What the hell is this?" I raised my arm finally bringing some attention to it.

"Your arm was fractured. We've got the X-Rays if you'd like to see them." Well, that wasn't really much of an explanation but it looked like it was all I was going to get.

"Shadow pack is no easy trek. If you'd prefer, you can lend my pack house while your Lycans fully recover and rebuild their strength." Those rumors were wrong; I knew that now. I truly felt sorrow for he was not a cold and heartless Alpha. no matter what was happening, or not happening, in his love life he had a big heart.

The clearing of his throat drew my attention and I sighed realizing I had yet again been caught dazing at him. It was the first moment I saw him smile and I couldn't help but be dazzled by it. "Yes, that would be very much appreciated."

"I'll have my people show your pack to their rooms and to the infirmary. And if you'll follow me I shall show where you'll be staying." His gravelly voice flowed through the air showing me great hospitality.

Caius led me out of the room and up the steps to the door. As I looked around I saw that all the cells were clear of my people. Stepping out the door I breathed in deeply as the crisp fresh air surrounded me. I followed Caius to a path that led into the forest. My head spun at all the colors around me.

We walked till the forest ended and opened up to a beautifully green grassy field. Past the field I could see houses, and on top of a small hill was a big pale brick house. That must be their pack house.

Caius personally led me into the three-story house on the hill pointing out the living room 'that way' and the kitchen 'this way.' I was too focused on the life that was emanating from the house itself. Photos and bright artwork hung everywhere, I could smell pasta sauce cooking and heard giggling and talking from all corners.

I didn't know why but I didn't expect it to be this way with one of the most dangerous packs in the world. It felt homely and warm. The pack house in our land wasn't much like this, it was more of a block of individual apartments with a big shared common room downstairs.

He led me up two flights of stairs before he stopped at an orange door. Now that I noticed it, I looked around to see all the other doors were brightly colored too. My mind may have been a bit too preoccupied with his jean clad butt to have cared what color the doors were, or anything else that was going on in the world. What could I say, he had very nice tight ass.

"Uhh. Why are the doors different colors?" I pondered looking around trying to clear my mind of his rear end, as he opened the door and showed me inside.

"We have a lot of children around, someone suggested to brighten the place up a bit by painting the doors. All the plain colors are guest rooms. Resident pack members mostly reside on the third floor but they all have name plaques on their doors as well." He smiled.

"That's sweet, and it really does brighten everything up. If my pack house back home was like this I probably would've spent more time there." I said as I got a good look around the room.

The bedroom looked like a hotel room. Bed straight in front of me with a window behind it and side tables on either side, chair in the corner, dressing table beside a door.

"That door leads to a shared bathroom, hope you don't mind. Just make sure you lock and unlock both doors when you're in there."

"No, that's not a problem. It looks nice." I was honestly just so lucky to have a bathroom at this point in time.

"Your pack has been brought their things, your backpack is still in my office."

"Thank you for that. Is it possible I could use the phone? I'd like to contact my aunt and uncle of Shadow pack."

"Of course, we'll go to my office; two birds with one stone." He was all smiles as he led me to his office.

"The phone is there on my desk." He pointed out the phone, "I'll just run your bag up to your room."

"Oh, you don't have to." I gave him a small smile.

"It's okay, I'll be back in a minute." I felt that was a surprisingly trusting and gentleman like gesture for this day and age.

I dialed Alpha Liam of the Shadow packs' main line and sunk down into a chair in front of Caius' desk; waiting patiently as the line rang. I looked around his office surprised by how nice it was. A theme of navy and grey with white furniture.

"Alpha Liam speaking." My uncle answered.

"Uncle Liam, it's Kira."

"Kira! How nice to hear from you, it feels like it's been ages." The excitement in his voice made me feel bad that I hadn't rang them in a couple of weeks, or to even have let them know about what had happened.

"Uncle, is it possible to speak to both you and Aunt Mary?" I'd rather tell them both together, I didn't want my aunt to worry about what was going on.

"Of course dear, I'll just go and get her." She must've been close by because it wasn't long until I heard her voice come through the receiver.

"Where's the speaker button Liam? Is she still there? Are you there Kira?" My aunt said making me giggle as I noticed Alpha Caius slip back into his office.

"Hello, Kira?"

"We're both here." My aunt replied.

"What did you need the both of us for? I heard there was a rogue attack down your way. Where are you? Are you hurt? Is everything okay?"

"Mary, let the girl speak."

"We were the pack that was attacked. It's a long story and I'll tell you when I get there. I'm travelling with what is left of the pack, we're heading your way now."

"Oh, my." My aunt gasped most likely hoping that her sister and brother-in-law were okay.

"Of course dear. You're always welcome here. We'll discuss everything once you get here. Will you be safe in getting here? How long until you arrive?" My uncle, always the controlled Alpha that he was.

"We should arrive within the week. We have stopped for rest at the Night pack."

"I knew that number looked familiar. Tell Lorena Matthews I say hello and stay safe honey." My aunt bid me goodbye.

"If there are any issues just call. We'll see you soon Kira."

I hung up turning to look at Alpha Caius, his eyes flicking feverishly across whatever it was that he was reading. His dark eyelashes fluttering handsomely as his eyebrows furrowed in concentration.

"Luna Mary of Shadow pack says hello to Lorena Matthews?" To this he looked up and I was glad to have had his attention again.

"Ah. My mother. They're close friends, have been for years. I will tell her."

CHAPTER SIX

AFTER SPEAKING TO MY FAMILY I left the office to visit the kitchen. I paused in seeing how crowded it was. While my people were occupied I decided it would be the perfect time to clear my head. Going outside for a stroll I ended up stopping at a small stream entangled into the woods just east of the house.

That was the spot where Caius found me hours later. He had been silently watching me from the bushes for about twenty minutes. I was sat on a large rock looking down watching the stream flow next to me. I'd made sure not to move or flinch when I first heard him sneak up on me.

"I was worried you had run off, I couldn't find you." I didn't turn to face him. My eyes would've been red and puffy. I hadn't noticed how they had been leaking until I heard him.

"What are you doing out here? Do you often stare off at nothing?"

"It's not nothing." I wiped my eyes with my sleeve before turning slightly. He had stepped out of the treeline and I tried my best to smile. "It's beautiful, was just getting too lost in my thoughts I guess."

I turned back to the sight of the river and slid across the rock to give him room to sit down. I continued to watch how the water softly flowed where it was supposed to. It knew what to avoid and exactly which curves to follow. I had always admired the beauty that naturally surrounded our universe.

I sat staring at the stream. I felt jealous that nature was there protecting the stream but had failed in protecting me. I knew my thoughts sounded crazy, but that was okay; I'd excepted my fate as a mate-less crazy cat lady.

I better start liking cats then, I giggled softly to myself.

"You're very odd, you know that?" I smiled and nodded at him in quick response.

"Why are you not at the house with your pack mates?" He asked and I turned my back on the flowing stream. "They'll be serving dinner soon if you're hungry."

"I needed some fresh air." I couldn't tell the truth, so I lied. It wasn't a complete lie I supposed, it just wasn't the only reason that he'd found me out here. I had wanted a moment alone, the pack house had been chaotic and I hadn't been able to think with all the going-ons. It had been a hectic week. There was only silence following my response.

"So, it's got nothing to do with what I overheard some of your girls saying?" He whispered making my head whip to him. I bit my lip because I knew who he was talking about and I knew what they would've been saying.

"It's all lies, they're just trying to spread gossip." I got up off my rock avoiding his burning stare.

"And I wouldn't know anything about that, now would I?" He said quietly, almost to himself but I caught it and paused in my escape. If anybody knew anything close to what I was feeling it was him. I'd rejected my mate, we'd been attacked by said mate and my parents had been killed right in front of me. But I still felt I had the better deal compared to him.

While the heaviness that had settled over my heart from my parents death had definitely taken it's toll, I knew I'd recover from it. I knew that I'd be sad but my parents wouldn't have wanted for me to just slump around missing them. I felt sorrow for him because he hadn't found his mate yet, my guess was that he may never find her. I squeeze my eyes tight shut before continuing my rush back to the pack house.

He replaced me as he sat staring at the stream, for a split second I could see the broken-hearted longing on his face. I wondered what he would've looked like if he was truly happy. I had wanted to hug him, like an injured puppy I had wanted to hold him in my arms and tell him it was gonna be okay.

On my way through the pack house I saw Dante entertaining some of the pack children in the living room. I stopped and waved at her feeling bad that I hadn't checked in on her or Carson. I stopped at the kitchen to make a quick sandwich and after grabbing an apple I dashed up to the orange doored guest room. I sat on the bed eating my dinner as I watched out the window at the few couples dotted around the picnic tables.

I ran a bath once I had finished my food hoping it would help me relax. I removed the bandage from the wound running from my temple down to just under my ear. It looked fine, it would definitely leave a nasty scar but it seemed to be healing right on schedule for a human wound.

Slipping into the hot bubbles was soothing but I couldn't shake the feeling that I was being pathetic. I didn't want to go near my pack afraid of how they felt about me. I was a mateless Alpha Female that couldn't even shift.

The bath started to turn cold and I knew my 'all relaxing' bath had been a waste of time. I hopped out and towel dried my hair before walking back into the bedroom. I noticed that the bedroom was dark, the sun must have set will I was soaking. I closed the curtains and turned on the light. My bag didn't hold much in the clothes department but there was enough to get me through a week.

I pulled on undergarments and an oversized t-shirt and some bed shorts. I jumped into bed just ready for the day to end. I had felt that way a lot lately, I just wanted time to pass as quickly as it could.

Sleep didn't come to me. No matter how many times I tossed and turned I wasn't to be granted the sanctuary of a peaceful rest. I sat up looking at the time, just past two o'clock in the morning. I groaned out in frustration, throwing the covers off my body I decided to wander around and explore more of the house. Putting pants on first of course.

I didn't stop my exploration until I came across the theatre room. It was massive and beautifully teched out. I picked out 'Narnia' from their extensive collection. I settled back into the first row of comfy couches and hoped the movie would soothe me to sleep.

"Kira?" I heard a voice call out. "What are you still

doing awake?"

"I couldn't sleep. Is it too loud? Did I wake you?" I panicked thinking I had woke him up.

"No, this room is soundproof. But I caught your scent and worried you might've gotten lost." Caius answered.

He sat down next to me on the first soft cream colored couch. He didn't sit so close that we were touching but close enough that I could still smell his delicious scent.

"Why are you awake?" I checked the time on the hanging wall clock, I read that it was close to 3 o'clock in the morning.

"Too much on my mind." He answered.

"Too many thoughts that just won't go away?" I stated. I knew that feeling very well.

"This was my favorite movie as a kid." I said not wanting him to think I had some crazy fetish for The Lion, the Witch and the Wardrobe.

"I like the third one the best. Don't know why, just always have." He replied.

"Why does everyone call you 'cursed'?" It had been silent for a little while and I finally found the courage to question the rumors that I had heard.

"Because I don't have a mate." He shrugged like it was nothing. No one just doesn't not have a mate.

"We're kind of in the same boat then." I said my mind not even processing what I was just spilling out to practically a total stranger.

"Why do you say that?" He asked but still fixated on the movie.

"Because, I rejected mine." He didn't say anything to

that, for which I was glad when the silence settled between us. We sat in the quiet, wallowing in self-pity and sorrow for each other. I had to admit it felt nice not to be alone with my pain.

I woke up in the theatre room, alone but the spot beside me was still warm and I was covered in a blanket. I couldn't remember watching the ending of the movie.

My eyes again flickered to the clock on the wall. It read close to half eleven. I got up, heading to my orange door on the second floor. I quickly changed into the only pair of jeans I had with me and freshened up hoping to rush down and catch Noah at lunch.

When I walked into the kitchen it wasn't as busy as I had expected. I saw three people working to prepare lunch for the packs but I only recognized one of them from my pack.

"Sammy? Do you know where Noah is?" I stopped the young pup from doing what she was doing.

"Alpha." She bowed her head. "Beta Noah is in the dining room with some of the others."

"Thanks Sammy." I smiled at her and left through to the next room. The dining room wasn't really a room; it was more like a hall. Three long tables where placed side by side surrounded by mismatched chairs.

The tables were occupied by lots of Night pack members I hadn't met, but at the end I saw a few from my pack gathered together. I walked over to them slowly as eyes turned to me. I assumed they knew who I was and what my pack was doing here so I only smiled in greeting. I took a seat across from Noah and Kathy as they stopped their conversation to welcome me.

"Hello Alpha." Noah smiled brightly.

"Alpha Kira, how are you doing? I haven't seen you around much." The ever-kind Katherine asked.

"Good afternoon Noah, Kathy. I've been... busy." I would have gladly told them that I was having troubles but not when we were surrounded by listening ears.

Kathy seemed to nod in understanding, "I'd like to meet with you both after lunch. I shall inform Alpha Caius and meet you in his office in an hour."

"Yes, Alpha." Their heads lowered as I left them with my instructions.

I exited the dining hall and headed to the kitchen to pick myself out some food. Rounding the corner, I crashed into someone, and I could now say moves like this should only be in the movies where it's nice and romantic.

The person grabbed me before I fell but that made him splash all of his pasta on me and spill a cup of juice at our feet. Needless to say, I slipped on it and pulled him with me to the ground. I yelped out as we went down.

When I opened my eyes, I was afraid of the destruction Caius and I had caused. Not to mention all the injuries I'd have from falling on hard tiled floor. Peaking my eyes open I saw Caius' grey eyes widely staring at me. Blinking both my eyes open I saw that I had landed on top of him, and I wasn't sure how.

"Was that your fault or mine?" He asked trying to contain the twitch of his lips telling me he wanted to smile.

I burst with laughing as I could only imagine what I looked like to him and what we looked like to other people. Both of us lying on the kitchen floor laughing like lunatics with juice and pasta everywhere. Luckily the kitchen wasn't overly crowded.

"Oh, my Goddess!" I heard a light squeal as heeled footsteps on the tiled flooring moved closer to us. I felt Caius groan from under me and pushed my uninjured hand into his chest to steady myself. Hmm. Very solid. My god, his mate would be one lucky bitch.

"Caius Killian Matthews! Why didn't you tell me you had found your mate?" The voice got close and I felt my body being thrown in the arms of a blonde-haired woman.

"Mother." He got up from the floor shaking out his limbs from the hard fall.

Woah, mother? She certainly didn't look old enough to have a son Caius' age. But I couldn't see too much, with her heels on she was almost a foot taller than me.

"I mean after all this time, and you keep it a secret from me. Do you know how long I've waited for this moment?" She scolded while a tear slipped down her face.

"Umm, Ms." I tried pulling away from the bear tight hug.

"Mother!" His voice had risen now and it seemed to get her attention.

"Don't raise your voice at me, Caius." I mentally laughed as he was still getting scolded by mummy at his age.

"Mother, you're hurting her." He said in a softer tone while unwrapping his mother's arms from me.

"And she's not my mate." My heart clenched at the thought. This time it didn't have anything to do with my mate but the fact that I'd loved to have been Caius' destined mate.

"Are you sure?" She asked urgently looking back and forth between us. I couldn't keep the slight frown off my face even if I had tried. I shook my head at her while giving her a small smile.

"Oh. I'm so sorry dear. My name is Lorena Matthews, I'm Caius' mother."

"I'm Alpha Kira Brookes."

"Oh, wow." She bowed her head, "Alpha." I smiled because her being a second-generation Luna meant she didn't need to bow to me.

"I heard we had another pack staying with us. Well I have to go, I just nipped over to pinch some tomatoes. You know how your father gets if there's not tomatoes in his salad." She laughed and started to stroll off.

"I'll see you again, Miss Brookes." She sent me a sly wink.

"Wow." Was all I could say as I turned to look at Caius head on.

"Sorry about that. She's a bit of a handful." As he ran his hands through his hair, his eyes closed.

"I'd call her spirited." I laughed as his eyes locked on mine.

We had stood staring at each other, my eyes were tracing along every one of his facial features.

"Oh! Um, right. I was looking for you. I wanted a meeting with you and my Beta soon, at one o'clock?"

"Let me get something else to eat, I'll change and meet you in my office." He smiled and I noticed then that there was slimy stuff in my hair.

"I think I'll go shower. This spaghetti does nothing for

my complexion." I chuckled and walked up to my room to wash the spaghetti noodles out of my hair.

After our meeting adjourned everyone went about themselves preparing for us to leave the next morning.

Most of the meeting had consisted of talking about maps and routes to Shadow pack territory. At one stage Caius offered to have us driven there but I had declined not wanting to put him out any more than we already had.

We informed the pack that we were leaving early the next morning, so they could prepare and rest up. The rest of our afternoon was about packing supplies and memorizing where we were going.

"Alpha." I heard a gentle knock at my door later that night as I repacked my backpack with my now, clean clothes.

"Mariella. What can I do for you?" I pulled open the door seeing the tall teenage girl from my home pack.

"Can I talk to you for a minute?" I nodded and opened the door wider to let her in, she seemed troubled. She ambled in and sunk onto the end of the bed.

"Is there something wrong Mariella?" I asked as I pulled up a chair and sat down across from her. Her unsteady breathing and mussed hair would've had anyone worried.

"I've found my mate, Alpha." She said in a low tone. From what I could recall she only just turned eighteen a month or two ago. She was a lucky one to have found her soulmate mate so quickly.

"Congratulations!" I offered with complete sincerity

and a wide smile. Just because I was misfortunate I still wished that others found happiness. "So what has you so bothered?"

"He's here, from the Night pack." *Oh.* It was very common for mates to be from different packs, but it did sometimes create conflict.

"Have you accepted each other?" I asked wondering what was standing between them in this specific case.

"Yes, but what now?" She questioned looking utterly torn. "What am I to do?"

"Well that's up to you, the both of you. You can stay here with him or he's welcome to come with us. If you're not ready then you can always give it some time, just cross that bridge when you've made up your mind."

"I'm allowed to stay here?" She asked sounding so surprised but timid.

"Of course. If that's what you want, we'll arrange it." Our pack had no problem with inter-pack transfers as long as my members were happy and safe. Plus, I knew she would be well looked after here.

"Mmm. I haven't told my parents yet." She whispers.

"Are you afraid they won't approve?" I asked knowing I would do anything I could to help her.

"No, but I'm their only child. I don't think they're ready to let me go yet."

"I'm sure they'll be very happy for you Mariella. I think you should talk to them."

"Will you come with me?" I laughed out but agreed and followed her to her parents' room.

After leaving Mariella hugging it out with her parents I

climbed up the stairs to the third floor looking for Caius' bedroom. At the end of the corridor to the left was where I finally found his name on a plaque nailed to a light grey door.

I quickly knocked twice not wanting to be caught in front of his door at this time of night, pack members might've gotten the wrong idea.

Caius appeared, opening the door wide enough so I could glimpse into his room, it was decorated similarly to his office. It also hadn't gone past my attention that Caius must have just hopped out the shower. His hair wet and slicked back while he was in long pajama pants and a zipped hoodie. His glistening tan chest slightly peeking out the top of his hoodie. *Hmm.*

"What do I owe for the pleasure of your visit, Miss Kira Brookes?" I giggled quietly but immediately shook myself, I was there on business.

I need to get a grip on myself. I didn't know what was making me feel this way but I was glad that we were leaving tomorrow and I could revert back to my somewhat normal self.

"One of my pack has found her mate in your pack. I came to officially request permission that she be transferred to your pack from tomorrow onwards."

"Of course, I wouldn't turn away mates. I will meet with her over the next week and plan the pack ceremony to introduce her." His heartfelt reply warmed the air around us.

"Thanks. Well that's all I had to see you about." Even though it came out of my mouth and I could hear my own voice I didn't move from my spot. That may have concluded my business here but I didn't want to leave.

"Goodnight Kira." He said in that soft lyrical voice of his.

I turned slightly to leave taking that as my queue of being dismissed, when I felt something warm against my cheek. His lips. *His freaking lips were on me!*

He pulled back but I couldn't look at him, I knew my cheeks were already on fire burning a bright pink color. I gave a sharp nod, eyes strictly on the door frame and then proceeded to run all the way back to my room.

My cheek tingled, and if I hadn't already met my mate I would've sworn it was a mating bond. I sighed dreamily leaning my back against my closed door. Well, that was the best bloody goodnight wish I'd ever had.

CHAPTER
SEVEN

A SMALL GROUP OF THE Night Lycans escorted us to the border at dawn, making sure we all left the territory safely. We travelled as fast as we could all day, across human lands. The pressure was off because we weren't invading anyone's territory but we made sure to be alert for wandering rogue wolves.

The pack was able to jog for periods of time, the warriors and higher ranking members carrying the small children of the pack. Everyone was generally in higher spirits; we weren't far from a permanent break and the pack had recuperated enough to push on faster.

I could immediately feel the change in air when we had past the border onto my uncles' lands. Since we were coming from the south east I estimated the pack house to be another half hour or so if we continued a walking pace. It had indeed been a long day; it was dark now but the glow of golden light in the distance told us that we'd made it.

The pack and I walked up the path to the pack house where I knew my aunt and uncle were waiting for us. It had taken a full day travelling to get there and the relief in the air was palpable.

"James said they're coming close now," I heard my uncles excited boom from afar.

"Shawn and Zoe?" My aunt called from under the porch lighting as soon as we were close enough to spot in the cover of night. She had been the first to notice that my parents were not there beside me leading the pack.

I shook my head and she was quick to pull me tightly into her embrace. The pack quickly started to merge into the pack house after learning the lateness of our arrival.

"Where's Warren and Lily?" I asked my aunt as we helped haul personal belongings towards guest rooms guiding pack members as we went. It was a surprise my cousin Warren, next in line for the Alpha title, wasn't there helping with pack affairs.

"Lily's at home, and of course Liam didn't want to leave her alone so he's made sure that Warren is home keeping an eye on her." She half sighed at the end which made me wonder if there was something she wasn't saying. I shrugged it off choosing to continue helping my people move into the pack house.

After making sure all my Lycans had places to sleep and knew where to wash up, my aunt and uncle pulled me away suggesting we ourselves head home.

It was so silent as we strolled down the short path to their private Alpha residence. I dreaded talking about it but I knew the inevitable was coming. So, in the dark of night after such a long time running, my uncle asked me, "Kira, what happened?"

I didn't know if the words would spell out of my mouth correctly. I took a couple of extra seconds and a few deep breaths thinking about the story I would tell, the tale of my parents' demise. I knew this was it, telling them, telling my blood family would be sealing my parents fate. Making it truer than everything up until that moment.

"I met my mate, a rogue. He attacked our pack with an army of rogues. We lost the lives of a third of our pack, including the Alpha and Luna."

"He killed them." I pretended that it was the brightness of the moon that was stinging my eyes and not the tears dying to be set free, but I knew the truth.

We had now paused on our journey to their home. I turned to face the couple embracing, my aunt silently sobbing into Uncle Liam's shoulder and Liam gently consoling her.

"My first thought was to come here; I knew the pack would be safe here. As we were travelling we crossed onto Night territory, unknowingly, where we were captured. Alpha Caius let us go once I had explained the situation, he then offered for us to stay and rest there."

"Oh, dear. Well, there's not much else to say except that at least you got here alright."

The house was deathly silent as we retired to our rooms, bidding each other goodnight with the promise to talk more in the morning. Thankful they hadn't asked about the bandage still in place on my face. I just hoped no one questioned it in the morning.

It had been such a long day. Hell, it had been a long week.

As I flopped back onto the guest bed I couldn't help but feel a sense of relief. The cold-blooded murder of my parents and pack members still weighed heavily on my mind as I took deep cleansing breaths but I felt the weight lessen slightly.

I could've effortlessly sunk back into the depressive state the rejection had put me in. It would've been so easy to let myself just drift back to that dark place. But, my parents wouldn't have wanted that. They would've wanted me to live my life to the fullest. To make everyday count, to live for them and honor their reputable name.

I sighed as I relaxed even further into the bed. We would work all the details out tomorrow, I dreaded the length of the day ahead but I couldn't help looking forward to reuniting with my cousins. *We made it, my Lycans are safe and sound. I hope to have honored my parents by leading our own to safety, I hope to have made them proud.*

That was my only line of thought as I drifted off into the deep abyss of sleep.

It was half five when my internal alarm clock woke me. I rolled and stretched before opening my eyes and noticing that I hadn't even changed my clothes last night, never mind actually getting in the bed.

Sitting upright I pulled off my shoes and quietly tip toed to the bedroom door. Peeking out into the hall it was still dark, meaning there was a good chance that no one was awake yet.

I tried to make as little noise as possible as I closed the door again, scooped up my back pack and rested it on the beds surface. I emptied the bags contents onto the bed and picked out some leggings, a target t-shirt and a zipper hoodie.

I was up now and since I knew for a fact I wouldn't be able to get back to sleep, I thought I may as well go for a quick morning jog. Us Lycans have so much extra energy naturally that we like to call ourselves hyperactive beings.

LUNAR ACCORD

I tied my shoelaces, grabbed my earphones and headed out the door. As I walked further away from the house a glow illuminated from one of the upstairs windows behind me. Inspecting it further I believed it to be Warrens room.

Nuts! I'll have to apologize for waking him when I return.

As I ran and jogged and ran again I noticed the sun slowly rise and the light overpower the darkness. My thoughts wandered exploring every inch, every darkened cornice of my mind.

Same old, same old. I hate to say it because I will forever be missing a part of myself that lived and died with my mother and father, but I just wish I could forget; forget about all the tragedy and loss. I was just so exhausted.

Trying my best to clear my thoughts I focused on the width of the trees around me, the green color of the leaves, the heaviness of my body as it pounded the ground with each stride.

Once arriving back at the house, bee-lining for the kitchen sink, I found myself guzzling glass after glass of water when I felt a tap on my shoulder. My heart shot out of my chest, my chest heaving with heavy breaths. I slowly turned, pulling out my earbuds, to see Warren standing across from me.

"Boo!"

"Are you done yet, you douchebag?" I asked my cousin, in fake anger, after a full minute of him looking quite literally like he might piss himself any second from too much laughter.

My heart rate normalized just before my aunt Mary strolled into the kitchen fully dressed and as put together as always. It has always puzzled me how Lunas were so perfect looking like all the time, I tried my hardest to always look nice but my style would never be up to that standard.

"Good morning dear. How'd you sleep?" She walked over and gave me a quick side hug her heels clicking against the kitchen tile.

"I slept fine aunty. I've been for a run; only just got back, though I'm not too happy with your son." I sent a pointed look Warrens way to see he'd started to sober up.

She followed my look to notice the state of her son as if only for the first time. "What's he done now?" she rolled her eyes and started to move around the kitchen picking up bits and bobs.

"He nearly gave me a heart attack, that's what!" I chuckled leaning against the kitchen benchtop as my eyes followed her around the kitchen. I don't think I'd ever noticed how she looked so much like mother, it was enchanting to watch her as she started cooking.

"Do you want some help to make breakfast?" I stood upright and shook myself enough to remember my manners.

"That'd be great, Warren you can help too!" She demanded. "So Kira, how was your run? You remember the trails okay?"

"It was very therapeutic. I remember the trails okay but I lost track of time, didn't realize how long I was out."

"Well you know if you need anything to just ask. I'm sure Warren would gladly take you to the new trail up near the northern border." She offered.

"Yeah definitely Kira you've got to check it out, it's through the northern hills. And don't feel bad if you can't keep up, there's signposts everywhere in case you get lost." Warren winked at me and in return I stuck my tongue out but to top off my ego aunt Mary laughed. We all knew it wouldn't be me that couldn't keep up.

Warren and I had always been quite close, even as children, seeing as I was only a few months older and we were both destined to be Alphas. I had countless memories of us growing up; racing, playing and even sharing Alpha training lessons.

"Warren!" We heard Uncle Liam's loud shout from somewhere within the house. I immediately cringed and worried as to what shit Warren had gotten himself into now.

Warrens face scrunched up as Mary turned to face him. "I suggest you run, my son." She turned back and casually resumed cooking while Warren ran off, toward or away from my uncle, I wasn't sure.

When it'd been a few minutes and the quiet still remained, I realized that I may have lost my mother and father in the rogue attack but my aunt had lost her family too.

"How are you doing aunty?" I continued to stir the batch of pancake mix that had been put in my care.

"It'll take some time to come to terms with having now lost both my sisters but there isn't much you can do. Just keep those loved ones in your heart and in your thoughts." She sighed out with a tight-lipped smile.

"We called Lily and Warren last night when you arrived to tell them about Zoe and Shawn. We've told them not to overwhelm you, but everyone will feel the effects from the loss of your parents." I appreciated the fact that I didn't have to say anything like I expected to. Of course, the time will come when I have to talk about it but I was thankful that I had a little bit of time to recover yet.

"I suggest you go wash up before breakfast, it's nearly ready." She said, but she was focusing way too hard on the food in front of her for me to believe she was okay. Finally, I relented in giving her some space to be alone.

"Sure thing, is Lily still asleep?" Referring to my other cousin.

"But of course dear, why don't you go wake her?" She chuckled. "Hey Kira?" She quickly stopped me on my way out. "I want to warn you that she's found her mate and you know how carried away she can get." She warned with a saddened nod.

I hadn't opened up to her about what had happened between my mate and I yet, I'd only been there twelve hours or so, but burdening her with my emotional pain wasn't something I wanted to rush. The rarity of my situation meant that no one knew how to react or what was to happen.

When the inevitable happened and I told my family the whole story of what happened, the reality of my future would set in. I believed the Moon Goddess when she told me there were great things in store for me, I led my pack away from danger to safety and with that I felt I could die fulfilled.

I just nodded and slowly walked up the stairs and to the right. I cautiously knocked then opened the door to see Lily laying on her bed; phone in hand thumbs moving a mile a minute. As she saw me her phone bounced on her bed and she came over hugging me tightly.

"I found my mate!" She told me, squealing in joy with a megawatt grin on her face.

She was an absolute beauty so whoever he was, he was incredibly lucky. My cousin Lily had shoulder length blonde hair, honey brown eyes and a smile that believed anything could happen. I quickly excused myself to the bathroom with the promise of being straight back to discuss details.

In the bathroom, I couldn't help but wonder what I should say, if anything. I took a deep breath before entering Lily's room. I noticed she hadn't moved from her spot on the bed, except now she was focused on the television across her room.

"So? Who is he?" I asked seriously although there was a small smile on my face, I then settled against the wall opposite her. I was truly happy for her but also felt I had to make sure she was okay and that he would take care of her.

"Oh, Kira, he's so perfect. His name is Scott, he's a pack member here in Shadow pack." She stated excitedly, moving closer sitting to attention.

"How did you meet?" I asked, keeping a still face.

"Well I was at Abby's house when her brother and his friends came home; he was one of them." She answered.

"Wait, so how old is he?" I raised an eyebrow at her. I knew that Abby had a twin brother but I was also sure they were older than Lily.

"Don't worry he's only 18. And he hasn't had mated anybody else, he said that he was waiting for us." Her and her inner beast all but swooned on the spot.

I was impressed, if he was telling the truth that is. The reason is, as soon as males mature and shift they develop an even more overactive sex drive. I'm not sure why that is but I know that if they can hold off until they find their mate, it's impressive and unfortunately very rare.

"That may be so but I hope that you're not just going to jump in the sack with him." I gave her a stern look, one probably only reserved for inquisitive mothers. I could only pray that she didn't have the same eagerness to be with her mate as I had with mine.

"Of course not," she said, lowering her voice suddenly appearing very shy.

"Good! Trust me Lily it's not worth it until you know for sure that you're ready." I gave her a smile sitting beside her on her bed to give her a side hug. It was only a few minutes of mindless chatter later that Aunt Mary called us for breakfast and we started to make our way downstairs to the dining room.

"So you said you were staying with the Night pack, how was that?" Lily started a more serious conversation as the family gathered around the dining table.

"Yeah, it was nice there plus I don't think the pack would have made it if we hadn't been offered the break from all the travelling."

"Did you meet him?" Lily suddenly exclaimed excitedly. "Well of course you did, right? You couldn't have been on Night territory and not have crossed paths."

"Who are you referring to?" I decided to play this out dumb, if I was right about who she was referring to I wasn't sure I wanted to discuss it.

"The 'cursed' Alpha?" she exclaimed again, this time her eyes widening as her voice raised.

"Lily." Aunt Mary spoke scolding her daughter for the insinuation that there was such a thing as a 'cursed' Alpha.

LUNAR ACCORD

"He's not cursed Lily." My voice was strained as I defended Caius' reputation and I knew that everyone had noticed it straight away. But, at least I had restrained from snapping at her; that's what my instincts were telling me to do.

"But isn't he like 30 and he still hasn't found his mate? Seems suspicious to me, that's like never happened in all of Lycan history!"

"Lily!" This time it was my uncle that sternly reprimanded her from his seat at the head of the table. "We have ties to that pack, don't be disrespecting their Alpha."

Unfortunately, at the same time a loud growl escaped me and I was sure I was more shocked than anyone else. You could only growl if you physically had a beast within you, which I didn't. Utterly puzzled with my own behavior I rashly apologized for my outburst and excused myself from the dining table.

))) ◐ ◐ ◖ (((

"I wanted to make sure you were okay. I didn't mean to upset you before. I was being insensitive and I'm sorry for offending you." Lily's voice called softly at me from the bedroom doorway.

The past hour or so I had spent sitting and staring, at anything; the lone tree outside the window, the clock on the wall across from me or even at the yellow birds printed on the wallpapered walls.

As my eyes rolled to my cousin and the sincere look upon her face, I felt incredibly terrible for causing her to have such a look of dishearten.

"It's okay, you were just going off of what rumors you'd heard. It's understandable that you're curious. I'm sorry for

97

snapping like I did." I opened my arms for her to join me on the window seat.

"Mum's just pulled a tray of cupcakes out of the oven, she asked if you wanted to help us decorate them. She was planning to take them over to the pack house hoping they'd brighten up someone else's day." The smile on her face as she sat beside me and spoke reminded me that she may not look much like her mother but they share the same hospitality and kindness.

"Sure thing kiddo, sounds like a nice idea." I stood and offered her a hand up.

"You know I'm not a kid anymore, right? I'm even old enough to vote now." Her expression was similar to that of a toddler stamping their foot. It was too cute to resist laughing; she may have been eighteen but she'd always be the baby cousin that I used to give piggy back rides to.

"So, is there anything you want to share with us, Kira?" Lily asked as we entered the kitchen to Aunt Mary mixing icing and Warren trying to get a taste of the icing.

"Like what?" I asked praying to the Moon Goddess she wasn't asking for specifics on my love life; the love life of mine that couldn't get any more non-existent.

"Oh, I don't know; did you make any friends in Night?" Warren butts his loud mouth in where it certainly did not belong with his remark.

"Meet any mates?" My other annoying cousin added in, and I swore I saw my aunt physically flinch at what she knew must be a sensitive subject for me considering the partial story I'd told her last night.

Despite myself being uncomfortable with the subject I lightly chuckled it off and replied that 'unfortunately' no I hadn't met any mates. They seemed to drop the subject easily enough when my aunty announced that the icing was ready to be dished out.

After icing only a handful of vanilla cupcakes I decided it was finally time to speak privately with my aunt and uncle.

Pulling myself to the mahogany door of my uncles' office I pulled in a deep breath and knocked three times as firmly as I could.

"Come in, Kira." His voice called from behind the door.

"Your aunt will be along in a minute." He jumped right to the point knowing exactly what my intentions were. I nodded silently in response and slumped onto the dark leather couch to the side of the room.

His office hadn't changed much from when I was a child; a few more books on the lone bookshelf, more files piled on his and a newer version computer completing the professional office vibes.

Zeroing in on my uncle sat behind his desk, he looked haggard and tired and I felt sorry for dumping even more work on his already loaded shoulders.

"How's Warren doing with his training?" I asked wondering if there was any chance that my uncle would retire early passing the torch onto his son.

"Right on schedule. Fortunately, he's in full time now so I can get more help around here." His lips tipped up to one side at the thought.

"Has anything happened that's causing more strain than normal?" I noticed his hair is thinning and there were bags under his eyes.

"No, nothing to be too concerned about. I look like this because of your aunt more than anything." His laugh boomed throughout the room only to be scolded down by my aunt herself.

"Well, excuse you Mister." *Oh, oh.* My aunt stood in the doorway, fists on her hips, a rubbish fake-angry expression on her face. She was so sweet looking to ever look too angry but it was cute that she still tried.

Before the ruckus started between the couple I started off I interrupted, "We're gonna need to shut the door for me to tell my side of the story."

My aunt closed the door and moved to sit beside me on the couch while my uncle set down his reading glasses and rolled his desk chair around to be in front of where I was seated.

"I'd met my mate at a party weeks before the attack. We'd hit it off, maybe a little too much, until we met again. That was when I noticed him as a rogue, we rejected the bond and each other right away." My breathing hitched as my mind conjured up images of that fateful day.

"You mated?" Mary's voice was as quiet as a mouse but still loud enough for me to distinguish the saddened note in her tone.

I only shortly nodded to answer her before continuing on, "When my parents found out about what had happened, my father started to hunt for him. I'm not sure for what reason exactly but when fathers' hunting party finally found the rogue armies' campsite they were spotted. We only had hours to prepare ourselves for the incoming attack."

My shoulders shook, the open window did nothing to help the shiver that ran through me. Throat tightening, I tried my best not to choke as I finished answering their unasked questions.

"My guess is that they would've attacked sooner or later, having seen our men snooping around just sped up the process. We lost a third of the pack including mother and father during the fight but my mate, the leader, is still out there. I knew we had to quickly move whoever was left of the pack as far away as possible."

A shaky breath left me as I realized that the worst part of the story, that hardest part for them to hear, was over. "We were lucky to have been captured by Caius and his pack. I honestly think my Lycans wouldn't have been able to make it this far without the refuge Caius offered us."

It was quiet and still for some time and it made the office feel eerie. My aunts tight embrace was the first reaction along with her disturbed breathing.

"I'm so sorry dear," she whispered her tight embrace tightening further.

"You'll all stay with us we could always use more Lycans around." Uncle Liam declared.

"Thank you Uncle." I gently smiled at him across my aunts' shoulder thankful for his help.

CHAPTER EIGHT

IT WAS LATE AT NIGHT. I'd been there a week and I knew that I desperately needed to leave. My pack would think I was abandoning them but they were better off here where they could be taken care of.

I was going stir crazy. I had given up my Lycans, they had now officially transferred to Shadow pack and it, safe to say, was starting to have some side effects. I was an Alpha without a pack, I knew that joining the Shadow pack was always an option but was just never something I could've considered.

The Alpha bloodlines were so strong, it wasn't something you chose, it was something born and bred into you. An Alpha without a pack was like a forest without any trees, it was odd. As a born Alpha it was within our primal instincts to lead and control our pack. Having them transfer to another pack had been painful, somewhat like a mate bond being rejected, our link was snapping.

Usually when two packs merged, or one conquers another, the Alpha Lycans battle it out. The winner became the superior Alpha and then led the pack, personally this wasn't an option for my situation. Other times one of the Alphas left with their family to live off on their own.

I felt guilty that I couldn't handle my responsibilities as an Alpha, a leader to my pack. I could only hope my parents wouldn't have been too disappointed in me for dumping our pack into someone else's lap. I appreciated what my Aunt and Uncle had done immensely, but I couldn't stay here long term and I wasn't fit to lead the pack on my own. That only left me with one option.

"Uncle. May I please talk to you, privately?" Deciding I only had one option and it was time to make that choice.

"You're not coping well, are you?" Despite needing to leave I knew I would always bear regret for leaving my family behind.

This past week had been a blast, surprisingly so, Lily and I spent quality time watching movies, baking, and even shopping. Warren and I had trained together nearly every day, I'd had a delicious array of home cooked meals and I'd spent time checking on my pack members.

One night I'd even gone around to Noah and Katherine's temporary residence for dinner. Everyone was just dying to sign the cast on my arm. They had known something wasn't right with my healing ability but they hadn't pressed for answer which put me at ease. It was so nice to be able to spend time with all the people that mattered most to me. It was almost too sad to say that I had felt like a ticking time bomb from the moment I'd gotten here. However nice my time here had been it couldn't compete with the fire inside of me that felt as if it was slowly being smothered.

"No I'm not, and I'm very sorry but I can't stay here."

I will admit to myself that it was a struggle to get that out but not to anyone else.

Carson and Dante's faces popped into my head as I recalled our conversation yesterday and their begging me to stay. It was crazy how quickly time seemed to have passed, it seemed like so long ago that my only problem was being rejected.

"Everyone else may not understand, but I do. What are you going to tell them?" My pack may not necessarily be my pack anymore but they were and always would be my family.

"Only the truth. Would you mind asking my father's council to come in, please?" My uncle picked up the phone to contact his new pack members.

I dreaded the knocking on the office door but was reassured by the smiling faces of Tyler, Kyle, John, Cameron and Noah.

"I'm guessing you'll have an inkling as to what's coming." I cleared my throat and stood tall to address my father's old comrades.

"I won't be challenging my uncle, which also means, I won't be staying here." My eyes wandered over each one of them individually. Noah was the most difficult one to look in the eyes, he'd been by my father's side since before I was born.

"You will all be safe here, I'm just sorry I won't be around to oversee you." My head tilted down letting my hair fall slightly.

I promised to try and visit when I could and threatened Tyler that he'd better take care of Carson and protect her. I was engulfed by hugs and farewells until only Noah,

Uncle Liam and I were left standing.

We each sat just talking and planning until past midnight. We discussed what I would do, where I would go and how I would get there. After reassuring them that I would keep in contact and visit whenever I could, I finally convinced them that I would be okay on my own and called it a night.

I had a few ideas as to where I would go or what I would do. There was absolutely no way of knowing where I would end up but I prayed to the Goddess that I'd get another chance to face my mate. This time I would be prepared, I would make sure he suffered a thousand deaths before finally dying. After rejecting me, taking my parents from me, and ruining my future; he at least owed me the pleasure of taking his last breath from him.

The next morning after heart-breaking goodbyes to my family and close friends, my uncle had insisted that him and his men at the very least drove me to the Night border. I couldn't say who it was hardest to say goodbye to but I knew the words Dante spoke would forever be engraved in my mind.

'I know how you've been struggling, I've seen it. But you need to truly forgive yourself otherwise the rest of your life won't be worth living. It's okay to move on.' She smiled the widest I've seen in so long with tears glistening in her eyes, I knew she was right.

When we arrived at the edge of the human lands I turned to Uncle Liam and Noah each giving them a hug and bidding them goodbye. I crossed onto Alpha Caius' territory hoping for a different outcome than the last time

I walked across those borders. It wasn't long into my trek that I was tagged by a small grey wolf.

"Alpha Kira, a friend of Alpha Caius.' I'm here to see him." I spoke firmly.

The beasts' eyes glazed over as he took in my scent. He must have recognized me, sure that I was not a threat as he soon shifted back to his human self.

"I'm Johnson, I have been instructed to lead you to the pack house." The boy said. I wasn't surprised that he'd been expecting me, my uncle had been on the phone with Caius this morning apparently.

"Thank you, Johnson." I replied as he started to show me the way.

As he led me through the lands I noticed things I hadn't last time. The beautiful houses, the tall trees and even the graveled path which led to the main pack house. Johnson knocked on the heavy oak door waiting only to alert someone inside before turning and leaving.

"Look what the cat dragged in." The tough nutted voice surprised me. I turned and looked up to see Beta Trent opening the front door.

"Well, hello to you too gorgeous." I said brightly to which he huffed at. "Where's Caius?"

"He's in his office. Up the stairs, second door to the right." He walked off leaving me with his half assed directions.

I walked up the stairs to see that one of the offices' double doors were open. I stood in the doorway looking at him, he looked so focused and in thought. The look of any busy Alpha.

I cleared my throat as I stepped through the threshold

and closed the door behind me. He looked up, startled from the paperwork scattered on his desk. "I wanted to say thank you for helping my pack last week."

"Alpha Kira, I wasn't informed you had arrived." The instant warmth in his smile sent shivers down my spine.

"Nowadays it's not often that strangers help strangers." I said, still referring to his kindness last week.

"You're welcome. Did you travel all this way just for that? You could have just phoned. Not that I'm not happy to see you, of course." I smiled as he joked.

"I was actually just passing through on my way back and thought I'd say goodbye." Well, it wasn't entirely a lie; I'd thought of saying goodbye but I'd mainly just thought about seeing him again since I'd left a week ago. It was all I'd been able to think about over the past week.

"Way back where? To your aunts' pack?" His face twisted in confusion.

"Back to my home lands." I said but internally winced at the thought of what my home lands would be like now. Remembering in that moment that I'd have to see Alpha Thomas of Crescent Moon pack about my lands.

Had they been utilizing it? Would it be housing rogues? Would it be completely trashed? I was curious but at the same time I feared the know the answer and what had become of my home land.

"Oh," He paused. "May I ask, why you're leaving so soon?" As he gestured for me to take a seat in one of the white leather chairs across from him.

"After the pack was attacked I wasn't thinking of myself or how I would fit in as a common Lycan of someone else's pack." I sunk into the white armchair releasing a whoosh of breath.

"Though I'm grateful, it turns out I can't let go of who I am just to fit into a pack."

He makes a humming sound as if to agree with my statement, "No Alpha could, it's programmed into our DNA."

We sat in silence as we contemplated our heritage. I looked around his office once again and was curious as to why it was so nice. It was unusual for Alpha's to have their main offices in the pack house, it was more convenient to have them in their homes.

"I live in the pack house; this is my primary office." As he seemed to have read my mind, my eyes flickered to meet his.

"Why do you live in the pack house? I thought you just stayed here last week to keep an eye on us." It was unusual for an Alpha to live so close to his pack. We had our own houses that were designated for the Alpha family. The pack house was for those that were unmated or unranked.

"I get lonely at my house. I was excited to finally have my own place when I became Alpha, I was so young then. It took me a while to realize that, that house was for my mate and I. It didn't feel right living there without her." Our eyes were locked and my heart broke slightly for him.

My eyes turned glassy, I tried my hardest to turn my attention to the window and calm my emotions. I would be the same when I went home, I would be alone. In a way, that was what I wanted. I felt as if I was broken and I couldn't stand being the poor broken Alpha anymore.

"What will you do when you're back home?" His voice was soft and melodically enchanting.

"I will repair the damage that has been done." Referring both to the pack lands and to myself. "Maybe I'll put my nursing degree to good use, maybe at the local human hospital."

"Right, well I'm going for a run before tea, would you like to join me?" He was so charming. My mind was so boggled at how someone could seemingly be so perfect when inside I knew he'd be feeling similar to what I had been feeling.

"I would lov-" I paused when I remembered my lack of beastly-ness. My eyes drifted low with the shame that I was a high ranked Lycan, without a Lycan.

"What's wrong, Kira? You can leave your belongings here, if that's it." He rose from his chair and rounded the table to be stood in front of me.

"Let's go." I said getting up before I had the chance to change my mind. "Do you mind if we don't shift?"

He seemed a bit surprised at my request probably because our beasts loved being out. He only nodded which made me sigh, he would know soon enough.

After locking up the office we walked down the stairs and through the packs living area. With each step I saw the looks from his pack; looks of jealousy, of pride, of happiness. There were so many emotions flowing around, I felt a bit tense. Everyone bowed their heads as we past and that was all that settled my insides, they didn't know that I was a failure.

We walked in silence following a trail that had clearly been trampled regularly.

It had been twenty minutes of comfortable silence between us amongst the forest when I chose to slice it,

"It's a full moon tomorrow night." Softly breaking the quiet with the obvious fact as the moon loomed over us.

Werewolves only changed on a full moon and that's why all supernaturals, including Lycans, are made to be alert on those nights. Because they can only shift during that period of time, their wolves can sometimes be wild and spontaneous.

"Does it still hurt you to shift?" He asked as we slowed our strides until we were just walking, his eyes looked over me and my very average stature.

"No." I replied simply not wanting to sound like I would welcome any further probing.

"Then, why don't you?" Obviously, my tone hadn't been enough to deter his mission. I decided to ignore my natural reaction to, basically, anyone else if they had asked the same question. His interest seemed so genuine that maybe it would be okay if he knew the truth, maybe he could be trusted with it.

"Because, I can't." As I admitted it aloud for only the third or fourth time, my voice seemed so small and weak.

"I don't understand." His grey eyes in the moonlight glistened almost silver.

"Those rumors you heard from my pack may have been partly true. Only my old council knows the whole truth though."

"Kira, please, I want to know." Again, if it were anyone else I would've ignored their pleading but it wasn't, it was the soft but daunting mateless Alpha.

"I met him at a party after the last day studying for my nursing degree. We mated straight away; I had been so worried about not having a mate that I was so excited that

I had finally found him." I stopped to break up the different parts of the sequence.

"I didn't realize my mistake until it was too late. The next morning, I found him again but I noticed something I hadn't the night before."

"His name is…" I paused having trouble saying *it* aloud. "He goes by Asher, Leader to the Rogues."

"I accepted his rejection easily enough but my Lycan hasn't made an appearance since." There's a long pause where the air around us becomes tainted with something I can't describe; maybe a mixture of shock and understanding but coated in thick intensity.

"Kira. I don't even know what to say." I didn't expect him to say anything, I wouldn't expect anyone to say anything.

"My father was hunting him but when they found him and his army it led us to the attack. Both my parents were killed, that's why I was travelling the pack to Shadow territory."

"He could still be there; he could be waiting for you." His voice took on that of a concerned parent or friend. I may have thought too much of it but it was sweet and unexpected from a stranger.

"There's the possibility of that, yes but maybe if he kills me he won't go after my pack." It sounded more morbid than I meant for it to but I spoke the truth, I would die if it kept my pack safe.

"No. Kira, please don't go. You could stay here? Hell, you could go anywhere." He was pleading with me not to leave but it'd be no different here than if I'd stayed with Shadow pack.

"I'm sorry Caius, but we both know I can't stay here, for the same reasons I couldn't stay in Shadow." Unfortunately, there was no way around that fact, no matter how much I would've liked to stay and get to know Night better. Not to mention their hot Alpha.

"At the very least will you stay a few days. I won't allow to you to travel when there are werewolves coming up to a shift. Otherwise, I'll be forced to escort you." His voice was challenging and I already knew I wouldn't win that argument. I simply nodded to appease his worried mind.

Just a few days. I can survive a few more days within a pack, I thought to myself.

We arrived back at the pack house the smell of pasta and freshly baked bread assaulted my senses and I realized only then how starved I'd been.

We'd sat alone at the kitchens breakfast bar to eat, thankfully avoiding the curiousness of the pack only one room away. Caius walked me to the orange-doored guest room that night but he lingered.

"Do you feel it too?" His hand softly grabbed mine.

I knew what he was talking about but it took me time to admit that these feelings we shared weren't real. Somewhere out there he had a mate; he would eventually find her and I would again be left on my own. Dating someone other than your mate was frowned upon and for good reason, we were born as two halves of a whole and jeopardizing that sacred bond was unfathomable.

"I...yeah." My eyes rose to account for his height looking into his eyes I saw a sparkle.

"I feel like I've known you my entire life," And yet my eyes reflected the regret my heart felt.

"Goodnight Cai." I let go of his hand and stepped away retreating to the safe zone behind closed doors. Before bed I called my aunt to check in on everything, she laughed loudly at my apparently overly concerned question. I couldn't help it, I was used to having people look up to me and my father. They had been my family for the last twenty-two years, they were to be my future before everything changed. I had a feeling some habits were going to be had to drop. My aunt and I talked for twenty minutes before we said our goodbyes and hung up.

Knock knock, knock knock knock

I'm jarred from a very peaceful sleep by knocking on the bedroom door. I wrenched the warm covers off my body and rushed to the door hoping to quickly quieten the ruckus. I ripped open the door and stood only half awake looking at a fully dressed and prepped Alpha Caius.

"Wow." The laughter in his voice and the humor clear as day on his face gave me much displease. "Well good afternoon Princess! You have a good sleep?"

"Please tell me you don't wake up this chipper every morning," I realized then that I was only covered by an off the shoulder sweater and booty bed shorts, they were very cute but not entirely appropriate. *Oh, well.*

Suddenly my thoughts darted to how Caius would look in the morning. Right after waking up, still in bed, naked and tousled. Maybe his voice was gravelly and deep with sleep. I held in a moan before shaking my thoughts off, they were heading in a dangerous direction.

"Wait. Did you say afternoon? What time is it?" *I never sleep past nine, how is it afternoon?*

"It's noon. And no I don't this is just a case of too much caffeine. But, I've had a brilliant idea." Now I was scared, the smile on his face was so large I thought it might actually split him in half.

"Why am I already feeling dread?" I couldn't help the way my eyebrows automatically furrowed together at his eagerness. *Wow, when did I turn so cynical.*

"I'm going to be in and out of the house for the rest of the day with business but I thought maybe we'd hang out later, yeah?" His smile softened but never fell.

"Sure." My too long fringe made a move to fall over my eyes making me run it back with my fingers.

"That is so not how you answer a very handsome young suitor that's knocking at your door begging to court you." Again, I just smiled at his silliness but I decided at the very least he deserved to be thrown a bone.

"Oh, my days! Of course, I will accompany you to the ball your royal highness."

"Much better. Be ready to go by 5."

"Go? Go where?" I asked utterly confused about how we went from casually hanging out to going out.

"It's a surprise." His smile twisted into a small smirk and his eyes twinkled with mischief.

I'm not sure what he's up to but he'd make one sexy devil.

"Caius! I haven't got anything to wear." I wasn't too worried because if all else failed I'd just wear what I was wearing now, but it had felt like the right thing to say.

"It won't matter what you wear Kira, you'll looked stunning in anything." I watched as he walked away and my face flushed.

CHAPTER NINE

THE LOUD KNOCK ON MY door at five o'clock on the dot got me thinking he'd been waiting outside the door until the clock struck five.

Since being woken up at lunch time I'd only left the room to make a sandwich, then I binge watched the first season of Friends and showered.

I started getting ready at four but since I was multitasking by also watching telly it took longer than normal to be prepped and ready. I still didn't know where we were going but I tried to be prepared for whatever tonight could throw at me. For a split second I felt guilty for wanting to have a good time tonight, both because he had a mate out there that he would eventually find, and because I had left my family and friends for a reason. I couldn't stay within a pack that wasn't my own and now here I was in Night pack.

I was currently washed, fragranced and dressed in a loose paisley blouse paired with skinny jeans and black flats. I looked cute but if I had to run for my life or shoot a basket I could.

Not sure what life threatening situation would call for me to play basketball but just for tonight it'd sure be embarrassing if I couldn't.

I opened the bedroom door slowly curious as to what Caius was wearing, which turned out to be jeans, a grey t-shirt and a leather jacket.

Damn it all if he didn't look hot as hell.

"Hey," I was suddenly concerned as to why my palms are sweating.

"You ready to go?" He asked, his eyes suspiciously rolling up and down examining my outfit.

"Yeah, all set." I turned to grab, well I paused because I didn't know what I was meant to take. I quickly stuffed some money in my pocket and picked up my jacket from the chair.

"You look nice." His smile lit up and caused his eyes to brighten slightly as I stepped out and closed the bedroom door.

"Thanks, so do you." And he *really* did. His t-shirt looked as if it had been sculpted for his chest, loosening off to hide the rest of his well-crafted body.

"So, how was the rest of your day? Are you busy with anything in particular?" I asked as we took to the stairs. He was an Alpha, so his work was something I was both interested in and familiar with.

"Normally, I wouldn't go into details about work this early on a date but since we're cut from the same cloth."

"Hey! What? This is *not* a date." My cheeks flamed with heat and I didn't even want to think about what I looked like at that very second. His chuckling didn't decrease as he walked ahead to open the door.

"Is it not? My mistake then." His smirk had my eyes narrowing closer to horizontal slits by the second. The door he held open led to darkness, I ignored every horror movie I'd ever seen and looked to him, simply raising my eyebrow.

Did he just expect me to blindly follow the crumbs to his gingerbread house? I wasn't sure, but I knew I fucking would anyway.

I stepped through the doorway and into the room, or what could be Mr. Matthews' Red Room of Pain.

The door closed and the lights came on a few steps into the room. It was a garage with four cars lined up in front of us. I didn't know much about cars but the line-up went blue hatchback, orange hatchback, black minivan but just behind the minivan was something I recognized specifically; a red Alfa Romeo Spider.

"Wow," I sighed out.

"Come on then." Cai took my hand from behind and started forward to the luscious red queen.

"In that?" I asked, not being able to keep the awe from my voice.

"Course, the others aren't mine." Like it was obvious that he wouldn't have had any car but the Spider. As he opened the passenger door for me I couldn't contain my giggles. I felt I should wipe my feet or take off my shoes before getting in, not wanting to look like a complete fool I simply slid in.

"Before, you were gonna tell me about work?" I asked as the car took to the road. I was genuinely interested in his pack work; I had missed it these last few weeks and maybe getting a whiff of it could tie me over.

"Yeah, that's right. Just meetings today; with my

council, one with Dawn pack and then I met with my architect." His eyes focused in on the road as we talked.

"Anything important I should know about?" I was pretty sure I was being nosy but if another Alpha was involved that meant there could've been something to worry about.

"Something you know more about then any of us." He paused building the suspense and my curiosity. "There's been rumors about the infamous rogue army; that they're recruiting. They've been spotted all down the east coast, it's making it hard for us to location their foundations."

"Ah," My ex-mate. "I'm sorry to say I can't really help with that, but my father's council would know more about their operations."

Just the thought of my old pack made me miss them. It had been a day and I already question my decision to leave. Had I really given it a fair shot over in Shadow? I regrettably knew the answer and knew that I had done what was best for everybody. Even if I could've handled staying, it would've confused my pack. My loyal pack mates would've continued answering to me. By leaving I gave them a chance to start over and fresh, giving them a new place to re-build their home.

"If you think it'd help then we'll happily get in contact with them, I'll set it up with Alpha Liam. All the Alphas are tense just knowing that there's an entire army of rogues out there plotting against us, especially since your attack."

"So, you met with an architect? Are you planning any big changes for the land?" Trying desperately to change the subject to something a little less doom and gloom.

"Not really. We're just having some work done on a few of the houses and I thought I'd throw some ideas around for my place." He said and I imagined what kinds of ideas he might've had.

"Exciting stuff, you'll have to send me pictures of it all when it's finished," because I won't be here to see it. I don't know if I say it to reinforce my decision to leave so soon or to prompt him to convince me to stay.

With the sudden lull in conversation the quietness and the low country music on the radio started off my insane boredom. I pushed a button on the console, the lit screen signaled there wasn't a disc in the player so I started searching the car for my music choices.

Pulling open the glove box I spotted CD cases; Nickelback, The Killers and Eminem. Interesting choices, not bad just not what I had expected but in being honest I wasn't sure what I was expecting. My eyes slinked over to study him as he drove; his wide frame pressed into the seat, his long legs slunk beneath the steering wheel.

Caius didn't have anything to say about my fiddling with his radio and for that I was grateful. I plugged 'The killers' disc into the drive and waited as it started to play. Unfortunately, that didn't appease me for long, by the four song I was bored and working on tapping a hole through my jeans.

"Are we there yet?" I rolled my head to the side waiting for him to answer.

"Will you chill the fuck out," he chuckled probably having noticed my angst.

"Fine. But seriously, are we there yet?" I didn't know where we were going and I didn't much care but we needed to get there soon.

"Soon." A noticeable tilt of his lips mocked me.

It's not even two minutes before Caius indicates off the highway and onto the slip road. Excitement bubbled in my tummy, we had to be close now.

After another few turns I saw it; the bright lights we were headed to. I twisted in my seat looking expectedly at Cai.

"We're at a carnival. You brought me to a carnival?" I found the situation strangely funny but he kept his composure playing it cool.

"Good detective work there." Sarcasm dripped from his tone making my mood flatten slightly. He pulled into a multi-story parking structure across the street from the fairground to find a decent sized space on the second floor.

"We used to come here as a family when I was little." We settled ourselves in the short queue at the gates to buy tickets.

"I'll pay for myself." I said as I noticed Caius trying purchase both of our tickets.

"I won't allow that." He basically threw the cash at the ginger teenage boy manning the entry booth to drag me away as quickly as possible. As we walked through the gates, the sun slowly setting and everything really started to light up.

"It's bigger than I imagined." The colorful lights flashed, the sounds of laughter and carnie folk calling as the smell of cotton candy exhilarated my senses. So much was happening all at the same time, it was all too much to wrap my head around.

My eyes were almost as big as balloons as we wandered around the park looking at all the different amusements. In my mind, I was already compiling a list of what I wanted to do. There was everything from hook-a-duck to a Ferris wheel to the roller coaster.

"What should we do first?" I asked as our eyes continued searching the vibrant scene in front of us. My eyes wouldn't leave the lone roller coaster as he said that I should choose.

"Definitely the roller coaster." So, that's what we went on. As we strapped in to our seats after lining up, the air became even more intense and electric. After a minute the safety checks began then we jerked as the ride surged forward. Off we went twisting and turning, up and down, then upside down; it was safe to say we were lining up again after the ride came to a stop.

After regaining my balance, stumbling for a bit, I asked Caius what he wanted to do next.

"Anything, you can pick." I squinted at him, was he seriously going to let me choose everything we did.

Shrugging, I simply nodded to the Haunted Mansion. After being completely bored by the 'Haunted Mansion' I pulled Caius up and headed to find the beloved Dodge 'Ems.

"That was so lame." Cai spoke out shaking his head with a wide smile plastered on his face.

"Yeah it was. How fake were those spiders!" My mind was so boggled as to how that was supposed to be scary. "Next up, Dodge 'Ems." I war cried while raising my fist in the air.

We had to wait in the queue for at least ten minutes before our turn came, we each jumped in a car and sat patiently while waiting for the whistle to blow. As I looked to Cai in the next car over to find his eyes already on me I laughed and stuck my tongue out at him, "You are so going down."

The rock music that played overhead got louder as the whistle blew and we set off to Dodge 'Em war. To say we were both competitive when it came to crashing into each other would be an understatement but it was all in good fun.

As time passed and we began to wind down from all out excitement, we finally decided it was time for some well awaited carnival treats.

"Thank you for this. You were right, I needed some fun. It's been a long time since I've been to a fairground." I said in all honesty as we stood in line at the food vendor.

"You deserve to be happy, Kira. You've had to deal with a load of shit lately but I wanted to give you a night of freedom." I guessed he was right but it felt hard to give that to myself.

After we stuffed ourselves with corn dogs, burgers and cotton candy it was time for our last stop before heading home; the Ferris Wheel.

We queued, strapped in then waited for the magic to begin. As we sat together across from a small boy and, what I expected to be his grandfather, our sides rubbed slightly before parting. My breath caught in my throat at the quick sensation of our bodies pressed together.

As the ride slowly kicked off I thought about how much of a perfect night this had been. I had to repeat to myself that it hadn't been a date.

But if it had of been, it would've been the best date ever.

The Ferris Wheel ride seemed too long most likely because we'd sat in awkward silence for most of it. The fact that we weren't alone, even though the carriage was roomy enough, had killed the mood for any personal conversation slightly.

There was still so much I wanted to know, to ask him. We'd had all night but it hadn't been long enough.

"The fairgrounds look so beautiful from up here, so bright." My eyes scanned all the booths below in wonder. Children running around with their friends; parents trailing behind, the odd petrified scream sounded above the bopping music and it was wonderful. I loved that in that moment I could feel the amount of life and energy around us with all of my senses.

"You wanna take a stroll along the riverside before we head back?" He asked.

"Have we got time?" I wasn't sure if we had to be back for a specific time or not, assuming he had work in the morning.

"All the time in the world. It's only nine o'clock." He laughed, "Do you have a curfew? A bedtime you can't miss?"

"How old are you?!" I laughed out at his immatureness. He had these moments of absolutely cheekiness that had made me question that a lot tonight.

"28. Why? How old are you?" He raised an eyebrow as if asking whether or not I was legal.

"I'm 22." I stated throwing in as much attitude as possible, mumbling a 'thank you very much' under my breath.

Shit. Wait, wow. Realization dawned on me that he'd been in pain way longer than I actually had been legal.

"That means you've been waiting for your mate for ten

years?" My heart saddened for him even more, it had only been four for me.

"It's been a long 10 years." He shrugged it off but I could see in his eyes how affected he was by all those years. I would've loved in that moment to have done nothing but console him and hold him tightly in my arms. Unfortunately, at the end of the day I may have been mateless, I may have been a weakened Alpha but I wouldn't ever be labelled a mate-stealer.

The soft lull in our conversation had given me time to think of other questions about him I wanted answered. "How long have you been Alpha for? I heard you were really young when you were handed the title."

"I was twenty when my father had an accident and wasn't able to lead our pack anymore." He didn't seem as concerned disclosing these details as I would have imagined.

"Is he…" I winced.

"No, he's still alive but he was in a coma for a while and became partially paralyzed." I had never met his father nor seen him around, I wondered where he hid himself away.

"How'd it happen? If you don't mind me asking." I asked anyway.

"A rogue attack." He spoke softly.

"Sounds all too familiar." I could relate to that and the pain the rogues bestowed on packs. Rogues weren't all bad to begin with but being a beast without a pack was something that severely messed with minds and turned those few into something extremely dangerous.

As we are asked to exit the carriage at the bottom of the Ferris wheel I started to like we had gotten somewhere tonight, that we'd grasped a new understanding of each other.

"Can I ask how you got that?" He motioned with his head to my face, the massive cut that wasn't quite healed yet.

"My mate..." His growl cut my sentence short. "He and my father were going at it, my father fell and I rushed in. I fought against him in my fathers' place but with me confined to my human form, he overpowered me."

"I can't even ponder the thought of it. To be so lucky to have a mate with such a radiating beauty and to literally tear at her. I wish I had been there, Kira." His voice was low and sad sounding. He was such a prince and I was thankful to have him to call a friend.

"What's it like, being an Alpha Female?" His question was a change of direction but a common question from outsiders.

Alpha Females weren't too common in our world because of our genetics. A thousand years ago all Alphas were naturally males, some ignorantly say that's the way it was always meant to be. Over time, as we evolved it started to become possible for strong Alpha couples to conceive daughters with the Alpha gene.

Of course, the ones who had conceived daughters tried again for sons, for they believed a son would be a stronger and a more appropriate option to someday pass the pack down to.

How incredibly sexist, but history was history.

My parents weren't the first to put their faith in having an Alpha Female as their successor but even in this day and age, it wasn't common among Lycan-kind.

"It shocks some people but a lot have come around to the idea and it's not like it's completely unheard of anymore." I'd never even noticed I was different until I started travelling to outside packs with my father.

"How was it for you growing up? Were you ever worried about ruling your pack?" He asked and I granted him answers only because I knew he was being curious not judgmental.

"Were you?" I laughed whole-heartedly at his question, of course I had been worried but every new leader is at some point.

"Good point." He chuckled with me, "I suppose what I meant was, did you ever feel being female would hold you back?"

"No." I could say confidently. "I was brought up to be strong, and fierce, and smart. The same way you were. I suppose I was blessed to have such a caring family around me, supporting me to no end."

I sighed as I pondered the loss of my family. It was a great honor to die trying to protect your pack, my dad would've liked that. I remembered that he used to say he didn't wanna die of anything boring. I had laughed, my mother had hit him over the back of the head for talking so morbidly. As bad as it sounded, I was glad they went together. It would've broken my heart even more to know that they were separated. At least I had closure in knowing that they were both together and at peace.

"I see that in you. It must be really tough to be without your pack" His smile was soft as his eye are downshifted onto the flowing river of water in front of us.

"Oh, wow, look at the moon; it's so full and beautiful tonight." I had only then noticed the moon, the reflection on the water pulling me to worship it. It was fully awake and had risen magically, showering us in its' natural light.

"Kira?" Cai called my attention away from the glorious glowing moon and on to him.

"Yeah?" My eyes locked into his, his gorgeous silver eyes almost tinted blue in the moonlight.

"Mate." Our voices clashed fiercely with the realization of the mate bond that tied us together. My mind blank, my heart full and my head feeling as if there were soft singing birds floating around it. *Cloud 9. This was it. The alleged fantasy land.*

Our lips locked instantly, heat burned through my veins but in the very best sort of way. His lips were soft and shaped to move against mine, to fit into me perfectly.

Having a split second of confusion I pulled away with my heavy breaths heaving my chest.

What was happening? This could not be real.

Catching his eyes brightly lit up tugged at my heart, no rational thoughts crossed my mind as a force pressed my body as close as possible to Cai's. We attached to each other as if our lives depended on it, and at that moment they just might've.

I stumbled back separating us as my body suddenly felt tired and very heavy, everything started to look hazy. It wasn't until the lights started to twirl that I felt my body fall to the ground.

My head landed softly, I opened my eyes to gaze up at the night sky, and I heard a soft mumbling but couldn't see where it was coming from. The pain started as I heard the first crunch of breaking bone, almost vomiting because of the sickening echo.

I couldn't process what was happening and I couldn't say that I wanted to. I only wanted to curl up in the darkness and be shielded from the blinding pain. It was a long time that I waited for the breaking to stop, for the hurt to end. For my body to run out of tears for me to cry.

I must have been a real site for sore eyes, I was not a pretty crier, something that hadn't really bothered me until this moment with Caius shadowing over me at my weakest.

My eyes sealed shut as an immense burning clawed at the skin covering my body. I felt it all. As much as I had wished repeatedly that I would just disappear, that I wouldn't be wide awake for my phasing into beast.

It would have been hours later when the trauma lessened, my vision focused for a second. That second was all I needed to spot those mesmerizing bright grey eyes I admired more and more the more I seen them.

I knew I was safe as I felt his familiar presence, I stopped fighting against the darkness that clouded behind my eyelids.

My beast has returned.

CHAPTER TEN

MY BREATH CAUGHT IN MY throat as tingles started spreading across my skin, once covering my entire body they started to stretch the width of my mind.

"Alpha Caius, good morning. Any changes since yesterday?"

"No doctor, unfortunately not." The saddened tone of the second male filled the air but with it came a fuzzy feeling within me.

"Her vitals are all normal, she's physically healed just fine. Give her more time, she'll wake up. Having been through so much and now..." The first voice spoke but zoned out as the darkness in my mind started to dance with shapes of color.

As I caught the shrill voices outside my realm of mentality I tried to focus in on them. They again spoke in sadness, making my heart beat stronger for them.

What had happened to cause all of this great sorrow?

The warmth that had been encasing my right hand suddenly left, quickly making my fingers twitch reaching to regain its blanket.

"She's awake!" The loud squeal may have come from a pig but I wasn't sure. "You really are her… you two really are…?" Soft sobbing followed.

The heat returned to my hand with electricity sparking its way up my arm. I mentally sighed with a happy fullness then started again to drift off to another land. Before my mind was completely lost the most beautiful melody stilled me.

"Kira. Can you hear me?" The voice brought my mind floating back wanting to be closing, to listen for more.

Kira. *Who was he talking to? Did I know them, the name sounded very familiar.*

"It's me. Please wake up for me." The warm voice was closer than before, right next to me. They were talking to me! I knew then that I would do anything to see if the face of the voice was as honey-like as their voice.

Feeling that the human body lying on the soft plush surface was my own gave me more incentive to rip through the cloud of fog that restricted it. At first I was happy that I could feel myself again, I could feel the slight ache in my muscles all the way from my toes to tips of my fingers up to my face and neck.

My fingers were all I could move, and only slightly, it felt like my body was trapped and I couldn't break free.

I wiggled, I shook, I twitched. Really trying to wake myself up from this fantasy realm; I wanted to go home. The same warmth that ensnared my hand made contact with my cheek.

"Kira." He called softly urging me to come closer. I gasped at the contact, the shockwaves that erupted were enough to relax the bounds on my body. I knew those tingles, that electricity and those shockwaves; and I knew who they were from.

"Cai." My eyes flickered open but slammed shut at the brightness. I moaned at the small pounding in my head from the light.

"The curtains are shut now, it's okay Kira." He stated softly, his fingertips gently brushing against my hand. I opened my eyes again, seeing Caius sitting on a chair beside me, still in a state of complete shock and awe. My eyes ogled him as my breathing hitched and my heart beat thumped loudly throughout my body.

"Mate," I whispered out. He nodded slowly as if reassuring me.

"Here," His voice was like silk against my skin. His eyes were more silver than grey but were tainted by the puffiness that lingered under them. He looked so tired, his clothes rumpled and his hair so stressed it was a wonder it hadn't turned grey yet.

I didn't know what to say; asking if he was alright seemed silly and saying he looked tired wasn't exactly a great compliment.

"Here, drink." I nodded softly and reached for the glass held in his outstretched hand. My hand shook slightly as the cool water slid down my throat. My eyes hadn't left Caius but then remembered we weren't alone in the room; the very unfamiliar room.

"Aunty? What are you doing here?" I finally noticed her standing at the end of the bed.

"How about I give you two some time and we'll talk later?" Her eyes were so wide and happy I could only have nodded in response.

"Thank you." Very grateful that she wasn't offended that I wanted to be alone with Caius.

"I'll go check where Warren and Lily are. We'll be back soon." Her smile was just as radiant as she winked and left through the open door.

As I took a second to regain my focus the first thing to ensnare my senses was the scent filling the air; fresh cut grass and apples. The second was the vision my eyes gave me as I glanced around the room. Everything was so crystal like, with intense color and sharp edges. The last thing I tested on purpose, trying to hear the birds in the trees outside.

She was back. I didn't know how it was even possible but I was me again, the old me.

Slowly my attention drew back to Caius' unmoved frame. I tried to recall my last memory before the darkness. I had left my uncles pack, I had come here, we had gone to the fairground.

And we had imprinted.

"How is it possible?" I asked utterly confused as to what, how and why. *Was it even possible?*

No, it's not, it couldn't be right? I'd had my one chance at love and I'd intentionally burned that bridge, wanting to cut all ties.

"The pull? It's so strong. How could it not be real?" I muttered more to myself than to Caius.

"It's real alright." His sincerity was what snapped my head in his direction. The determined look in his eyes told me he was convinced.

"We're… soulmates?"

"Yes." His small smile tried but couldn't contain what his eyes told me; he was happy too. I'd never seen that look on his face before, without that layer of disappointment and heartbreak he looked younger. My heart stuttered in my chest, it had been all I'd wanted since I met him.

"But how? Caius, you know I already have a mate..." His fierce growl caught me off guard and the tingles of arousal it pulled from me was also a mighty surprise.

"No, your bond with him was broken. Your bond with me is something entirely different." He huffed out.

The knocking on the door caused our eyes to drop, "Alpha, Luna Mary notified me of Alpha Kira's awakening. May I check on her?" When I looked up to inspect who it was in the doorway there stood an older man in a light blue shirt with a stethoscope hanging around his neck.

"Yes you may, Doctor...?" I beat Caius to the chase as I welcomed the curly haired doctor into the room.

"Please call me William, Alpha. William Tate." His smile showed off his teeth as he cautiously entered the room and rounded the other side of my bed.

"So Alpha Kira, how are you feeling? I've cut off your cast and taken off the bandage of your face. Both injuries have healed right up, you're as good as new." He asked as he inspected the monitor beside the bed.

"I feel great. My muscles are still a bit achy but I expect that'll soon go away. It's true that I shifted?" I asked only to just realize I would've been naked after shifting back.

My hands flew to my chest but under the covers I was fully decked out in my pajamas. Flicking my eyes to Caius he at least had the decency to avoid eye contact, I puffed out a breath. At least I could trust he wouldn't have had anyone else seen me in such a vulnerable state.

"Yes it is, I bet you're over the moon about that." His smile turned sympathetic, "You're all clear, so as soon as your muscles recover you'll be free to resume all your normal activities."

"How long have I been out?" I asked as the doctor started to untether me from the heart rate monitor.

"You shifted and fell unconscious two days ago but we've been monitoring you very closely just to be on the safe side." He next started to fiddle with the IV stuck into my arm and the drip stand next to the bed.

"Two days…" *Hmm.*

"Call me back if she starts experiencing any problems." William nodded to Caius.

"Thank you William," Caius dismissed the doctor just by the finality in his tone. As the door shut and we were left alone once more, the air crackled with unspoken emotion.

"There's more we need to figure out, about us but we'll discuss it later."

"Okay," I was petrified of what more would come, and was totally unprepared for what we could possibly have to deal with.

"How about I run you a bath then get you something to eat? It's nearly lunchtime." I felt my mouth water a little at the thought of food but pushed it aside enough to answer him.

"That'd be great Cai, thank you." He squeezed my hand before standing upright.

"Anything to make you feel better." He answered as he

moved around the bed to what I guessed was the bathroom.

As I had a few minutes to myself I finally took an intensive look around the room, I noticed that there was a frame on top a grey chest of drawers against the far-left wall. But that was the only personalized trinket I could see in plain sight.

I gently lifted myself up into more of a seated position before swinging my legs off the edge of the bed and standing up. Fully upright I could feel the ache in my muscles all the way down to my bare feet.

Moving and retrieving the picture frame from the drawers I inspected it closer. In the photo, there was a couple stood in front of a large cream bricked house, in the mans' arms a small child; a boy.

Was this Caius as a child? The thought made me smile to myself. The startling resemblance even from such a young age was spectacular, everything from the color of his hair to his facial structure, but the eyes of the child were the most familiar; the color of melting silver.

"Kira, the bath is almost ready." He called out from the bathroom where I could hear the running of water.

"Cai?" I popped the frame back where it belonged and moved to stand in the bathroom doorway.

"Who's room is this?" Closely my eyes followed his every move as he pulled a towel from one of the alcove shelves. The grey tiled bathroom didn't explode much color except for the blue and red towels and a few bits plotted around; aftershave on the counter, body wash in the shower, toothbrush in a holder by the sink.

Cai coughed clearing his throat before answering, "It's

mine."

"In the pack house?" I wasn't sure why it was so important to me, probably because I knew he'd saved the Alpha house especially for his mate.

"Yes." *Phew*. I felt as if I wanted us to talk about our mate bond, understand what it meant before we jumped down into the valley of mate-hood and crossed that threshold. Pun intended.

I had slept, bathed and eaten. I was now beyond bored and all I could think about was the fact that my beast had awoken. After I'd bathed and Cai had sat with me while I ate, I sent him away. I knew that he needed to rest before resuming his pack duties so I basically had to force him out the door. I wanted to be outside; beast ruling me, wind breezing through my fur as I ran and played.

Not being able to handle my beast clawing at my skin anymore I sat upright wired with excitement. Ripping the covers off I flew over to the window opening it and checking its distance from the ground.

Yep, third floor window.

Taking a deep soothing breath, I stripped off my bed top and shorts readying myself for the shift. I heard creaks coming from down the hallway and froze; at any second someone could enter having found me looking like I was trying to run away.

Now, I've got to jump now!

I leapt through the open window as his significant scent wafted up my nose. Shifting in mid-air as graceful as I'd ever been made me smile with pride inside. Silver fur surged from my skin as the rest of my body took only seconds to reshape itself into that of a wolf.

"Kira!" The loud cry as I landed with a thump on the grass had my head swiveling to look back at the window.

Indeed, it was Cai at the window; a blood stricken look across his face. My playful yip was to calm his uneasiness before I shook out my fur and stretched.

Everything was so new but in an odd way still somewhat familiar, like from a past life. I sprinted off in the direction of the biggest tree cluster, I knew Cai would follow me but that did nothing to dampen my beasts' urges. Despite wanting to be close to her mate she also wanted to be free of any human restraints.

Hell, I wanted to be free too. I'd had enough rest; I was starting to feel the effects of claustrophobia being caged in that room and it had been less than a day!

I knew Cai would catch up to me soon but I chose to enjoy frolicking around his land in the warm sunlight for as long as I could. The slight wind that rustled the nearby trees made luscious sounds and felt cool against my fur.

As I slowed my run to a jog the loud growl behind me drew my attention. I hadn't seen Caius in beast form before so this was a big moment for me, one I had been so looking forward to.

Caius' midnight fur matched his human hair color while mine was the complete opposite. What really, caught my eye was the colored patches on the tops of his paws. Matching to his eyes and my own fur he had patches of silver fur covering all four paws.

My jaw dropped, the sight of him was enchanting; his beast was large, quite normal for an Alpha. I, myself was only slightly smaller than him; the total unfairness of being a woman. I may be the picture of equality being that of an Alpha female but nature still had a hold over us and our abilities.

We stood there, not far from the packs village, face to face. I assumed we were waiting for someone to bring us clothes.

In the meadow, a few people milling about began to stop and stare at us. I could see the confusion on his packs faces as to who I was, which was understandable; I wasn't linked into their pack and having the air of an Alpha meant I could've been a threat to their leader.

To make more of a scene then I was used to, I slowly stepped up to Caius. My eyes lingered on his, our intense stare unbroken by anything; not even the pack doctor, William, arriving with our clothes. Once close enough I nuzzled up against him simultaneously zoning out from the peers surrounding us. He was warm and welcoming and oh, such a comfortable place to lose myself.

The applause and laughter that erupted from around us proved to be enough to startle the spell we were under. I grinned as much as I could still in beast form all the while stepping back. Caius' eyes shone with pride and happiness for a split second as his pack appreciated his new mate.

As my eyes were scanning the crowd Caius had shifted back, his naked glory not on show for long enough for me to admire it as he quickly pulled on red Nike basketball shorts and a white t-shirt.

"Everybody, please return to your activities." His voice coming across stern but the smile on his face softening the Alpha laced order.

While the crowd quickly retreated Caius became solely focused on me. He took the clothes offered to him by

William before he too vanished.

His voice wasn't raised but very rough as he scolded me, "You shouldn't have run off like that, you've been out of action for a few days; you should be taking it easy. You could have hurt yourself." He softly sighed.

"Your uncle has arrived and he'd like to meet with us. He was the one that found, what he thinks to be, specific information on us." He said outstretching his arm in passing me a bag full of clothing.

I wasn't as brave as he was, I hid behind the nearest tree as I shifted back to my human self and clothed myself with jean shorts and an extra-large hoodie. I would change in front of anyone else but coming to him, it was different; I was shy.

"After I brought you back to the pack house, I talked to a few of our allies, asked around for information about anything that could help explain this." He continued while we started our short march back to the pack house.

"And, did they find anything? There must be some explanation." I couldn't begin to imagine what explanation there could've been for me being bonded to two Lycans.

"Your uncle sounded quite confident that he found something worth looking at but we'll know more when we speak to him." His tired tone almost sounded bored, *where the hell did his sudden attitude come from?*

The brisk stroll to the house was silent, and awkward; I wanted to feel his skin against mine again. We had been friends, I would've said, before we called 'mate' but now, it was like our whole relationship had been tilted.

"There's a prophecy," My uncle spoke quickly as we stepped into Caius' office where Liam had been waiting. I gasped in haste at the shared insight; those things didn't usually end well for anyone named in them. Uncle Liam flicked the book rested on his lap open to a certain page then thrust it at us. Cai accepted the book examining it closely as he hunkered down in a chair next to my uncle.

As I looked over his shoulder at the book I couldn't help admire the full page black and white drawing of the moon goddess, it was a close call to how she had appeared in my dream.

The opposite page had 'Bound' written across the top of the page and below it read in cursive print; "'One rejected, one cursed; will merge as one whole. Stronger than all, but built for longer. Linked to the moon goddess, her mistake will be her redemption.'"

"That's us?" I looked over to my uncle for an answer, a simple nod of his head.

"I've spoken to pack historians, past Alphas, councils; they all believe you two could very much be the Moon Goddesses' Bound soulmates." Well if it were true it didn't seem too doom and gloomy, thankfully.

"Is this all the information you could find?"

"So far, sources up in Canada could have a better understanding of it." He was speaking of The Elders. The Elders were older generations of powerful Lycans; including descendants of the Royals' Council. They had no influence over us but they were very knowledgeable.

"Of course, The Elders." I nod along in thought. Father had always said that if anything were to ever endanger our species that The Elders would've been the first place to go for information and guidance.

"We'll plan a trip to visit them over the next few

weeks." Caius said, more to my uncle then to me. I wasn't sure why he was acting funny with me but I was not going to go away; no matter how much he dismissed me.

"I have some calls to make, I've been informed your family is waiting in the living room for you." Before Caius had even finished his full stop, I was holding the door open for my uncle.

"I'll show you where to go, Uncle." If I remembered the way that was. After Liam stepped out into the hall I closed the door softly after him.

Glaring as hard as I could I stood tall, facing Caius. My voice low I spoke as threateningly as I could, while still having warm gushy feelings for the man in front of me. "I have a few choice words for you later."

I spun off my hair flying out behind me, and slammed the door so brutally behind me, I was afraid it had splintered the wood. My uncle stood waiting for me trying to hide the smile threatening to show.

"Sorry 'bout that." I knew he'd been close enough to hear through the door with his heightened senses.

"It's okay love, how about we go spend some time with the family." His arm wrapped around my shoulders and we whisked ourselves away to the pack house living room.

CHAPTER ELEVEN

"KIRA," MY AUNT EXCLAIMED upon seeing me. "Look at you! No cast, no bandage. I'm so glad you're all fixed up. How are you feeling? When Alpha Caius informed us of what happened we came straight over."

"You've all been here since Tuesday night?" I asked completely awed and shocked.

"No, unfortunately I've been too busy to visit but your aunt and cousins came to check on you every day." My uncle explained.

"Well, you should all know I very much appreciate it." And I did, I was beyond thankful that they cared so much for me to bother.

"We're just glad you're okay Kira." Warren shared his concern, with Mary, Liam and Lily nodding in agreement. After sharing hugs, we settled down to talk about everything that had been going on; the time I'd spent here, how worried Caius had been and our mate bond.

"I'd just like to say that I totally called it." Lily pointed out; proud of her, totally non-existent, psychic abilities.

Of course, she and Warren still didn't know about my first mate, the other one that I had rejected; nor would they ever find out if I had it my way.

"So have you two discussed it yet?" Aunt Mary asked as I wished the conversation to be over and for the brown leather sofa to swallow me whole.

"In a sense." The bright smile I forced on seemed to be believable but the sly look I received from my uncle told me otherwise. Okay, so I was fibbing, *hard,* but I didn't want to give her any cause for concern.

"That's good dear, you deserve to be happy. Maybe you'll settle down and have a few kids. We could come and visit more often, or even babysit." As her excitement only increased so did my dread.

)❯❁❀❁❀❁❀❁❁❁❁❁❁

Hours later, when Cai finally emerged out of his office, he came to find our little clan had moved our reunion to my old guest room and were half way through watching Finding Nemo. His scent caught my attention then I heard him stop outside the bedroom door. He stayed there a while and with no one noticing I used my ninja skills to slip out into the hallway.

And as I had predicted there he was, stood in front of the bedroom door looking ruffled. We stood a foot apart in complete silence staring at each other. I was upset with him but I also wanted to pull him closer, to soothe his troubles and make him happy. I needed to know what his deal was, what was wrong with him.

"The Elders were a rather closed book about the whole thing but said they'd look in to it pending our arrival." As he trailed on I found myself not actually listening to the words he spoke but carefully watching the way his full lips moved as he spoke them.

In that moment, I couldn't care less about The Elders, the prophecy or any of it. None of it mattered until we sorted ourselves, and our relationship, out.

"Do you not want me as your mate? Are you wanting to reject the bond?" Damn, I'd been through it once and somehow lived to tell the tale but I knew I wouldn't survive rejection a second time, no doubt about it.

And, I didn't want to.

Suddenly his face cleared of all tension he had been holding on to. "You think I've waited all this time, put up with being 'the cursed Alpha' for you, just to reject you?"

"Well if you want me, why don't you act like it?" My tone had risen and I felt apologetic for anyone that I had disturbed. When mates first made contact with each other they were drawn in like magnets, why was he fighting the pull instead.

"Because," His stubborn voice rose again, sparking my annoyance more.

"Because what?!" We stood, facing off, in the very public hallway but I didn't care. I was upset, I was angry and I was frustrated that we weren't getting anywhere.

"Because. I've been sprinting towards the side of a cliff for a long time ready to jump but now that I'm finally at the edge of it, staring right at you; I couldn't be more terrified Kira." And just like that, my heart was torn up, all anger forgotten; left in its place was only sadness.

He was scared. And with that final thought he walked away from me, leaving me frozen and staring after him.

My family left me soon after; it was getting late and they

had a long journey home. I was still scorned from my argument with Caius but I wasn't sure what to do about it. I could've just let him come around to it on his own or I could try and push him to accept it. To accept our destined relationship.

He wasn't the only one that was scared. I had somehow been lucky enough to have been granted a second chance; I wasn't prepared to blow it. But the difference was, I wasn't willing to jeopardize us just because I was afraid. Life is about more than just being alive; it's about living, facing your fears and making the most of the life you've been given.

It was late at night; I was half way between falling asleep and being wide awake. Feeling the bed dip behind me perked me up. The tingles I felt as an arm wrapped around my side told me who it was. I relaxed as Cai pulled me back against his chest. That was the first night I fell asleep in Cai's arms and I knew I would never want to fall asleep anywhere else. The next morning, when I woke up the bed was cold and empty. It was at that point that I had decided that I needed to talk to Caius.

When I did talk to him I, myself, needed to be ready for the shit that was going to go down.

So, after a late breakfast seated at the breakfast bar in the kitchen I roamed around the pack house a little more. As I rediscovered the laundry room I made a mental note to do some washing soon. I didn't have much in a sense of clothing so it was a priority that I kept on top of my washing.

Maybe I'd go shopping for more clothes soon...

"You're our new Luna. You're pretty." I had found myself on the well-worn porch swing out the back of the pack house when the little girl appeared at my side. Kids were at school; most adults were at work so the only people still around were the young pups and their parents. I must've been zoned out while soaking in the beautifully bright sunshine.

The little girl in front of me might've only been about three or four, with bright blue eyes and brown pigtails hanging over her shoulders. I suspected that she'd come up from the playground where the other children were playing.

"Sophie!" A frazzled young woman walked up behind her, "You can't just run off like that sweetie."

"I hope you were being nice," she spoke to the little girl, "I'm so sorry Luna. Come on Soph we'll get you some juice." Besides me not knowing what to say to Sophie, she hadn't been bothering me. Although I had always wanted a big family of my own, children still stumped me.

'Luna.' Hang on a minute.

I stood quickly from the swing to follow them inside, their scents leading me right to the kitchen.

"Luna?" I asked the woman, startling her. "You called me Luna?"

"Yes."

"Why?" Just because I was Caius mate didn't automatically make me Luna; there needed to be an announcement and a ceremony. Besides, the pack hadn't even been officially told of me yet.

"It spread quite quickly through the pack that the 'Alpha Female' was Alpha Caius' mate. People said they saw you claim him and him accept you. Is this not true?"

Well, shit.

"Your information is correct; I just hadn't expected it to travel around so quickly." Her shoulders slumped, clearly with relief.

"We've been waiting a long time for Caius to find our Luna. It's a very joyous time for all of us." She opened the steel fridge door and pulled out a juice box.

"I'm Mia White," she held her hand out to shake. I took her hand in mine for a gentle shake before releasing, "and this is my daughter, Sophie." She nodded her head to the little girl sitting on a bar stool then slid her the juice box.

"It's very nice to meet you both, I'm Kira Brookes."

"So Kira, how are you settling into our pack?"

"Okay I think, everyone seems pleasant enough." The obvious choice was to lie; I wasn't going to say that her Alpha had been a bit of a dick to me or that I hadn't actually met any members of the pack accept for Dr. William and Lorena, Caius' mother.

"Everyone is quite open and friendly but there will be a few for you to be wary of." She flicked her fringe out of her eyes and in that moment, she looked the spitting image of Sophie.

"What do you mean?"

Was there already people that didn't like me? That are against my bond with their Alpha? There couldn't be, I hadn't bloody met anyone yet!

"Nothing new, just the same old sk-" Her eyes flitted to her daughter and mine followed, a smile broke on my face as I saw Sophie's cheeky grin. It was almost like she knew her mother was about to say a bad word and she was just waiting to catch her out.

"Let's say there are some very 'popular' girls that

wanted desperately to be mated to our Alpha." She rolled her eyes and huffed. "They're out to gobble up every and any one of high ranking. Very pathetic, very unoriginal."

"Should I be particularly worried?" My eyes narrowed and my head tilted with the underlying current of my words.

Was Alpha Caius a man-whore that had anything to do with 'those' girls?

"No! Goddess no." She rushed then laughed out. "He's not like that."

Thank the Moon Goddess!

"By any chance, would you know where I could find Luna Lorena?" I asked. I had an idea that maybe Lorena could've helped me with Caius.

"Yeah of course, Lorena and Phillip live down in the village. Would you like me to show you there?"

"If you could, but I wouldn't want to impose."

"It's no problem, I'd feel honored to show our new Luna around." She winked and walked around the counter to pick up Sophie.

We started our journey by walking across the field of luscious green grass out the back and to the patch of trees that gave added privacy to the pack house. The pathway was paved through the woods until the trees grew sparse and continued down a housed lane. The main street was up ahead and I knew I'd seen this before, when I'd first arrived.

Quaint store fronts outlined the road; a few clothes shops, a fruit and veg store, a florist etc. As we passed by the bakery I could help but reminisce to Mia about my old town and how Dante's family had owned the bakery;

A.K.A our local hangout. Mia was remorseful but reciprocated, pointing out the burger joint that was her high school hangout.

The more time I spent talking to Mia the more I found how much I'd missed my friends and that I liked Mia. *Definitely friend potential there,* and that thought brightened up my entire day.

Turning off the main street we came to a slow stop at a white brick bungalow with a wooden fence and a very well maintained garden. It was modest and homely. "So, this is it. If you need me you know where to find me, maybe we could arrange to go out for lunch one day next week?"

"Yeah, I'd like that. Thank you, Mia." I smiled at my new friend.

"To get back to the pack house just walk back through the town, follow up the path we came on and that'll take you right there."

"Okay. Bye Mia, bye Sophie!" They both waved before turning and continuing on their way.

As I knocked on the solid white front door of Caius' parents' house I didn't expect his father to be the one to answer the door. We hadn't actually met yet but I stood there praying for him to approve of me.

"Hello Mr. Matthews. My name is Kira Brookes," I stuck my hand out to shake. "I was looking for Lorena."

"I know who you are dear. Come in come in." The twinkle in his eyes gave me hope, "Lori! We've got a visitor."

"Well, who is it dear?" She called back from somewhere further inside the house.

"One Alpha Kira Brookes to see you." Their

conversation was playful and sweet, building my fondness for the couple. It felt familiar; like being home again.

"Kira!" Lorena squealed as she made her way into the front foyer embracing me tightly.

"How are you doing? Since Caius sent out that order not to bother you I've had to force myself not to go near the pack house; I know how over-excited I can get," She chuckles.

"Caius did what?" He had sent out an actual order for no one to disturb me. It was the sweetest thing and the dumbest thing anybody had ever done for me; at least the thought behind it must've been genuine.

"I'm taking that you didn't know."

"No. So that's why it's been so quiet." A small revelation spoken mainly to myself.

"Is there any particular reason you came to visit, dear?" She spoke as we moved to a beautiful cream couch decorating the front living room.

"I was kind of wanting to talk to you." Not wanting to sound rude in excluding Mr. Matthews.

"Phil, it's girl talk, you're dismissed." She bent and kissed his cheek before he started to roll away.

"Lovely to meet you Kira, hopefully we'll be seeing more of you from now on."

"It was nice meeting you too." I called after him as he disappeared from my line of sight.

"Don't let his cool fool you, he's been dying to meet you. Now, what's up?"

"I was hoping you might be able to help me. Things between Caius and I haven't been running all too smoothly and I want to change that. But, I'm just not sure how." His moods had been running so hot and cold that I wasn't sure what was going through his head. I knew he was scared, I was too, but wouldn't we be worth the risk?

"Oh, dear, what's happened?"

"He's been distant since that night and he says it's because he's scared, but scared of what? I'm willing to fight for this relationship but I can't know how to fix something if I don't know what's wrong in the first place."

"Ah. I think that might have more to do with what happened to his father than anything. When Phil was attacked and in that coma, he was there for weeks. Cai would sit and wait for him to wake up but more so, he watched how much that incident broke me." She took a breath before continuing. "Everything turned out okay in the end but I had always wondered how much that might affect his relationship with his own mate."

"He's scared to lose me like you nearly lost his father." It made a hell of a lot of sense.

"He came to see me, not for long but I think he just needed reassurance that you'd wake up."

"So, what should I do? Just talk to him?" At least I now had an inkling as to what had been halting the progress in our relationship. He most likely didn't want to get too emotionally detached in case I ran off or something happened.

"Well just between us girls, tempting a male's sexual desires opens them up, makes them vulnerable."

"Really? You're telling me to use my body against your son?" I couldn't stop the barrels of laughter that shook my belly to its very core.

"Yep, he might even be vulnerable enough to let down his defenses and let you in. It's not the most conventional method but it'll definitely work." She winked and I had to pretend we weren't, in that moment, talking about her son.

After finally making my way back to the house I noticed more people milling about than before. As I passed by I got a few nods, a few whispers and a few skeptical looks; all of which I ignored.

On my way to my prison cell of a bedroom I scented Caius from outside his office door. As far as I'd known he'd been out most of the day. I could feel myself wanting to stop, to see him behind that door. The itch to be close to him was rising to an uncomfortable level. I held my breath as I continued on; desperately seeking the solace of my bed.

Wild thoughts ran through my head as I quickly pulled on my sleep clothes and fell onto the queen-sized bed. It was late in the afternoon, I had time for an hour or so nap before dinner.

Was he purposefully avoiding me? What did he expect me to do? Did he even really want me? Was my time being wasted here?

Eventually the headache my thoughts had given me won out as I propelled into the deep dark ocean that was sleep.

Taking in to account my very early night I wasn't surprised to have woken up at half four the next morning. It was after ten minutes of being awake that I realized I hadn't eaten dinner last night causing my stomach to suddenly growl and moan to be fed.

Trying not to make any noise I tip toed across to the door out into the hall only to stop at the staircase. It wasn't so bad creeping around the second floor because nearly everyone on the third floor would've still been asleep. But stairs, they had a history of creaking under any shifts of weight.

Very slowly shuffling down the stairs, by the time I'd made it to the bottom turbulence free I could've screamed with joy. On cloud nine and feeling like I was crushing life I walked into the tiled kitchen.

Flicking the light switch on I startled from the menacing sight of Caius stood over the sink with a bowl of cereal in his giant hands.

"Cai? What are you doing up?"

"Been having trouble sleeping." The dark look in his eyes told me I might've had something to do with that. I was just surprised he answered me at all. I moved to the fridge and pulled out the eggs.

"Yeah? You should try some warm milk before bed." I reached for a coffee cup getting ready to make a proper breakfast. I didn't know how else to respond, I hated that we were apart, especially at night but it wasn't keeping me awake. I think the Moon Goddess had messed with enough of my life, she wouldn't want to mess with my precious sleep too.

"I'll try that," I mixed two eggs and a splash of milk into the cup and stirred. As the silence between us grew I threw my focus onto anything I could.

Coughing erupted from Caius as I went to grab the bread. "I should go get ready." My eyes swung to see him walking backwards to the kitchen entryway. "You might wanna hurry before someone sees you, *like that*."

That bastard! What the hell did that mean, that I'm so blindingly ugly it'd offend the early risers?

LUNAR ACCORD

My fingers automatically combed through my hair, it was somewhat tangled and in desperate need of a cut but it wasn't any messier than usual. If only I'd had a mirror to check myself over but by reaching into the back of the fridge for the butter I caught a cool draft. That's when I noticed I was in my night clothes.

Well, maybe the bastard had a point. It wasn't the best attire for greeting people first thing in the morning. It annoyed me even more that he made a fair point.

I had been sorting through my clothes when a knock sounded on my door later that morning.

"Hey Cai, what's up?" I opened the door to see Caius stood on the other side of the threshold. He was fresh looking in his white button up shirt and dark wash jeans.

"Your cousin Lily has been on the phone. She told me to pass it along that she's coming over to visit today."

"Okay." He lingered. "Is that all?" I wasn't trying to be rude there just seemed like there might've been something on his mind.

"No. Yes. Look, I'm sorry okay?"

"For what?" I knew what he was sorry for. But it's one thing for me to know and completely another thing for him to know. I leant against the doorway waiting for his answer.

"For being so harsh with you this morning, and for everything else." The 'everything else' bit wasn't the most direct route for an apology but I'd accept it as a general sorry for being an asshole. His broad shoulders were sagged. His whole demeanor changed him, this was not the man I first met a few weeks ago.

"It's fine, how about we talk about it tonight?" I really didn't want to be getting into this now. I wanted to do it when we had the time to sit down and talk properly. No interruptions, no escapes. Just the two of us free to finally talk seriously about where we stood in our bond.

"Okay. I should be in my office all day today so if you need anything just let me know."

After my chat with Lorena yesterday I had been inspired to win him over, by whatever means necessary. Even if that meant turning to the dark arts of sexual manipulation, I chuckled at myself, as if that'd ever fix our problems. Though I did like the idea.

CHAPTER TWELVE

IT WAS LITTLE AFTER TEN o'clock in the morning and I was sat flicking channels on the telly in my room, ready and waiting for my cousin to arrive. I'd hoped we'd go shopping, so I'd been busy making a mental list of what I wanted. I needed clothes mainly but I wondered since I'd be here for the foreseeable future if I should look for other stuff. Some things to personalize my bedroom, maybe DVD's or photo frames maybe even some wall paints.

The only problem was; would I be there or in with Caius. I secretly hoped that there would be no point in putting personalized touches on this room.

"I'm going out." I announced to Caius as I barged into his office soon after Lily and her mate Scott arrived. I was surprised at the appearance of Scott by Lily's side but I was glad she was happy and that she wanted to introduce us. Scott was only a couple of inches taller than Lily with dull brown eyes but he had the most gorgeous blonde shaggy hair. He seemed very laid back and quiet but you could tell he was totally smitten.

"Where?" He dropped his pen on the table and directed

his full attention onto me. I had obviously interrupted him from his paperwork. *Oh, well.*

"East Haven Shopping Mall." Apparently, it was the closest mall and of course Lily promised she knew exactly how to get there. She was somewhat of a shopaholic I had to admit.

"Here, use it however you like." He stood from his chair, pulled out his wallet and handed me a credit card. Insulted to the max, I revved my engine and went for him. How dare he insult me that way. I was an Alpha, I had my own money. Just because I was his mate did not mean he would have that hold over me.

"Seriously? Un-bloody-believe. Here, use it to go screw your-" Coughing from outside the office door interrupted me; I sighed at the interruption. *Maybe I'd better just cool my jets; I think he might've been trying to be nice.*

"I've got my own, thanks anyway." I mumbled and kept my eyes down as I turned and exited the room.

"I think you may need some cough drops, I'll make sure to pick some up for you." My smug smile was challenged by her cheeky grin as we linked arms and skipped away from Caius' office.

We hadn't even reached the staircase when I felt Cai following us. As we walked out the front door I couldn't resist glancing back at Caius, he was stood in the doorway of the kitchen watching me. Goosebumps rose on my arms as our eyes met. In all our drama, I hadn't had much time to just stare at him. I wanted that more than anything, just to freeze time and appreciate every fiber of his being. He was beyond gorgeous, the definition of tall, dark and handsome.

I'm glad we were on speaking terms but it still wasn't

enough, I wanted more. I wanted a mate and a relationship, why was it so difficult for me to have both.

After nearly a full day spent with Lily and Scott I couldn't stand the sight of them anymore; which was why as much as I loved her I was glad to see her leave. We had shopped, eaten even seen a movie; and it had exhausted me. They were so much in love that they were unknowingly sickening to anyone within a five-foot radius. Today that had been me, and I had never felt so much like a third wheel in my entire life. It only proved to remind me how much I wanted it to work with Caius.

I dropped my bags to the floor in my room and flopped on the chair. I still needed to talk to Caius but I didn't know where he was. Truth be told I couldn't give a shit about looking for him, he'd find me when he wanted me. But for now, I had bags to unload and sort through.

At the mall, I decided against looking into the home décor shop, the room was nice enough as it was and it had all the essentials I needed for the time being. I looked around, it was basic but all I needed for now. *I hoped it was just for now.*

Just like I had predicted Caius came knocking about an hour later. I'd finished my unpacking and was on to reading a new book I had picked up at the mall earlier that afternoon.

I simply opened the door wide enough to let him in and resumed my spot in the chair. I needed to finish that page, I couldn't just stop reading in the middle of the couples very public argument.

"Sorry. I'm done." I placed my book mark and put the book on the desk beside me. Looking around Caius had closed the door and was now seated on the bed facing me directly. I took a deep breath, "We need to deal with this Cai."

We couldn't hide from our relationship any more, it was becoming too difficult to run from the inevitable. "Caius, I can't stay here and keep resisting you any longer. I've tried to give you as much space as I can but it's becoming physically impossible."

We both sat; him thinking over my words and me taking in as much of his delicious scent as possible. I needed to be closer. I stood and walked to Caius settling down on the floor in front of him.

"Caius, regardless of what anyone else thinks, our souls have recognized each other as mates. We were made for each other…" His grey stormy eyes speared through mine and I was possessed. I couldn't look away.

He slowly leant forwards and down toward me. I couldn't control the way my lips gravitated towards his, the way they sizzled and reacted to his kiss. Just as I remembered, his lips were soft like marshmallows but firmly meld to mine as we pressed closer together. This kiss was different than the last we'd shared; this was slow and controlled. It was us conveying our acceptance of each other. The fact that he initiated contact made me believe that this could work, that we could have a fully functional and loving relationship.

"I'm ready." Cai pulled away slightly creating much needed space between us for the heat in my cheeks to cool.

"Ready for us?" My mind was still a bit jumbled by the kiss but I needed to make sure we were on the same page.

"Ready for all of it. I've not known what to do about our situation, I've been afraid and I haven't handled it well." He hadn't really handled it at all, but I felt it probably wasn't the right moment to point that out. This was going better than I ever expected although I still wasn't sure where we went from here.

"How about we start fresh?" I suggested. It'd have been better if we had started at this point when I'd first woken up but I'd take anything over nothing at all.

The smile that lit his face almost brought tears to my eyes. I made that smile appear just by accepting him in my life as my mate. More than anything at that moment I wanted to reassure him about his worries and insecurities. The excitement and happiness that whooshed through me may have made the rash decision but I stuck by it one hundred percent.

"I'm so sorry, Cai." I was high on life and the ecstasy that was us accepting each other. Being away from one another had weighed down heavily on the tie that linked us together.

I knelt up nearly eye level with Caius. When my sight slid to his neck I felt my canines lengthen. My beast was rising to the surface and I couldn't stop myself from sinking my teeth into his neck; racing ahead to mark him as my own.

As my teeth pulled out of Caius' skin his sunk into mine, making my eyes scrunch tight at the sharp pain. I grabbed onto him as my legs turned to jelly. The euphoric waves came and my hands clutched at anything and everything they could, wanting just to pull me in closer to him.

"Kira." Cai's voice whispered in my ear. He sounded out of breath. My eyes opened to look in to his burning silver orbs. The realization hit that I just marked him as mine was striking. Trying to stand on my own two feet proved to be more difficult than previously thought as he held me up against his body.

"I wanna show you something," He spoke as he gently placed me back on the ground. As every inch of my body fizzled and warmed with his touch it was all I could do to nod my head. My eyes blinked hazily before I felt myself being lifted. Sharply looking to Caius my arms made their way around his neck as he held me bridal style.

"I can walk." Stubborn as ever but I wished I hadn't open my mouth, I didn't want to walk. I wanted to be in his arms for however long he'd hold me for.

"You look tired." At least it matched the way I felt.

"Kira." I must have dozed off on our journey but I felt Caius' voice vibrate against my neck.

"Welcome home, Kira." I was shocked as my eyes flickered awake to take in our surroundings. He walked, still carrying me, through black iron gates and slightly up hill on a wide gravel path. The house stood in the distance was gorgeous, any little girls' dream house. A white two story farm-style house with grey paneling. Coloums were holding up a roof over the porch that ran along the front of the house and around one side, a garage attached to the other side.

When we got to the steps leading up to the porch I jumped down out of Cai's well muscular arms. I faced him clasping his hands in mine.

"This is your place?" It looked like everything I'd ever dreamed of.

"Our place." As he spoke my arms wrapped tightly around his waist and a lone tear slid down my cheek eventually falling onto Caius' shirt as I pressed into him.

LUNAR ACCORD

From that night onwards our lives would forever be entwined.

))🌑🌒🌓🌔🌕((

I felt the pillow beneath me move ever so slightly. I held on tighter to keep the warmth all to myself before trying to drift back into my deep slumber.

The pillow pulled away again, my hands roamed around groggily looking for the source of movement. The warm muscles under my hands had me thinking that I was still in dreamland. Finally giving in and opening my eyes, I saw the sweltering silver pools of my warm pillow.

Caius?!

I jolted away as his gruff voice filled the still air, "Good morning."

Sat upright, I turned to look at Caius lain spread out next to me. I tried to remember how we got here but was distracted by the sight of Cai, my mate, laying shirtless in a sea of the white cotton sheets.

He was gorgeous, with a face carved by angels and a body sculpted for only Greek gods. His broad frame looked even bigger from this angle. The ridges of his toned abs set in deep. His biceps bulging as he rested his hands behind his head, my breath caught in my throat. I'd never been this close to his barely clothed body, it was the first time I'd gotten to inspect him closer.

Looking at his every feature I noticed the smile on his face shone something between mischief and pride. He was happy I was checking him out, but even more pleased to have caught me doing so.

"Where are we?" I hoped the change of subject would give my cheeks time to cool. I finally tore my eyes away

165

from Caius' tremendously gorgeous body long enough to look around the room. Finding my surroundings, unfamiliar my eyebrows scrunched together in confusion.

"We're home." The weight of the sentence shook awake my memories of last night, of us marking each other and of Caius showing me the house. Of him and I finally accepting each other as soulmates mates.

"You remember…?" Cai sat up next to me gently running his fingertips over the sensitive skin of his mate mark on my neck. Bared for all to see for the rest of our lives.

I nodded, shifting my eyes back to him. "How'd I get here?"

"You fell asleep as we sat on the porch. I carried you to bed." To bed. To our bed. In my mind, I did a happy dance, elated that I'd have my someone special to share a bed with.

"Thank you."

"I'm sorry if I woke you, I was getting up for my morning run."

"It's fine, I usually wake up early. Would you mind if I joined you?" My inner beast was scratching to be free again, but this time it wasn't to feel the freedom. She desperately wanted time to bond with Caius.

"I'd like that."

We both moved to get out of bed. "We'll have to wear our clothes from yesterday. You'll have to let me know when you're ready to move your stuff in. I'll be packing my things today but I don't want to rush you into anything."

"If this is too soon for you, it can wait." He continued and my appreciation for the man in front of me shot through the roof. He'd been alone so long and even with all the delay between us already, he'd still happily wait for me.

I walked over to him and standing on my tip toes, I wrapped my arms around him. He was so sweet to offer but I was more than happy to let him know that it was full steam ahead from now on.

"I'm ready. I want to be with you, I'm all in Cai."

"Good. Me too."

We made our way to the front door and stepped out onto the porch. The sun was lighting the sky but only softly. "How about after our run we go to the pack house and start packing. We'll come back later and I can give you a proper tour of the house."

Cai saw my nod seconds before we quickly stripped off. Although I wasn't comfortable being in so little clothes in front of him, I pushed my unease to the side. I kept my eyes down, away from Caius' tan sculpted body and unleashed myself, leaping forward landing on four large paws. I was already taking off down the driveway when Cai phased and followed after me.

Cai saddled up beside me and I let him lead the main pack house. The soft rustling of grass underneath our feet was all that echoed in the morning woods. The more we continued on deeper into the trees the more my angst continued to grow. Catching Cai's eye, I noticed he was on alert too.

I howled to get Cai's attention at the first breath of danger. The scruffy grey rogue that barreled toward him caught my attention immediately as I looked over to Cai beside me.

Cai swung around catching the rogue and using his strength to toss him into a nearby boulder. Suddenly, the rogue was not alone. I fell forward from the unexpected weight but quickly started bucking against the wolf that sat on top of me.

Finally freeing myself, the second rogue wolf rolled off of me. I faced off with him as he hastily got to his feet. His face was scarred and torn up, and I felt sick to visualize all the different ways he'd been tortured. The blood thirsty look of his red eyes had me snarling and lunging forward. My teeth snapped at him, aiming to land into the flesh of his furry neck.

It wasn't long before the cavalry show up to collect the bodies, among them I spotted Trent. We knocked the intruder's unconscious with ease, only keeping them alive enough to be interrogated. Everyone was a little on edge as we followed behind the warriors carrying the limp prisoners. For two rogues to come out of nowhere to attack an Alpha male didn't sit right with me, or anyone else, there must've been a specific reason.

Maybe it was a suicide mission.

No one, not even crazed rogues, would attack an Alpha without any major back up. Never mind attacking two Alphas, a very strong Alpha couple such as ourselves. Though being quite random the thought of our combined strength led my mind to wonder what our children would be like.

But... Did Cai even want pups? He must, he'd need an heir to take over his title eventually. What if he didn't, I had always wanted a big family; being an only child had that effect on me.

My eyes unconsciously wandered to Caius as he walked beside me. Realizing how stupid my inner turmoil sounded

I shook myself away from it. We had only just settled as mates, there was no way I should've even been thinking about this yet. We had plenty of time but also plenty of other things to work through first.

As we neared the steps to the underground prison cells Cai quickly pulled me back, stopping me from going any further.

"You don't need to be here for this. I'll meet you back at the pack house." My first instinct was to scream and protest but as I locked my eyes on his I could see him silently pleading with me. I sighed, I didn't want to cause trouble when I knew he was only doing what he thought was necessary to keep me safe.

"If you need me…" I let the promise hang in the air as I turned and let one of his council lead me to the house. Every step further away from Cai tugged on my heart strings. I wanted to be with him, by his side every second of the day. We had already wasted enough time being apart.

Arriving at the pack house and making my way up to the orange door, I knew that sooner or later there'd need to be a conversation about his Alpha male attitude. I wouldn't ever be able to just sit back and watch as he ran the pack, I wasn't built to be just a Luna and he needed to know that.

The first half an hour passed at snail speed as I paced back and forth around the room. I sooner snapped, finally having had enough; I started pulling together my things ready to move into our new house.

That was where Caius found me when he finally graced me with his presence. I asked how everything went before he had even fully closed the bedroom door. I may've been slightly on edge.

"We didn't get much out of them." *Oh*.

"Are you finished packing?" He asked quickly switching topics.

"Yep. What about you? Are all of your things ready to be moved?" Even as I spoke I had reservations about us moving out and over to the big house. It might've been safer for us to stay within a group environment if there was going to be more rogue attacks. But, on the other hand, we couldn't put our lives on hold just because a few rogues had turned up on our lands.

We made our way up to Cai's room on the third floor to finish getting his things packed. He didn't have much in the way of knick-knacks or personal touches so it didn't take us too long.

"Are you sure about this?" I asked, yet again.

"Yes, he's sure already." Trent bellowed as he walked up the porch steps and past us, boxes resting in his arms. I didn't blame him; I had asked this at least five times on the drive over and we were only in the truck for a maximum of ten minutes. Still, I rolled my eyes at him before turning my attention back to Cai.

"Yes." He softly chuckled at me but his smile was all the reassurance I needed. His arm slipped around my waist and he used it to pull me closer to his firm body.

My hands rested on his chest and my forehead fell to his shoulder, we stood there for minutes. It was silent between us but I loved having that time to just breathe him in. His skin was so warm underneath his t-shirt, his heart thumping steadily in his chest. Inhaling, his scent had a warming and calming effect on me.

"Barf." *Immature ass*.

"Trenton Xavier Grand." I looked over at the new voice noticing that Cai's mother, Lorena was standing about twenty feet from the front porch and thundering towards us.

"That is your Luna you're speaking to. Show some respect boy, you wouldn't want your parents thinking they didn't raise you right." I loved this woman. I looked to Trent who stood in the front doorway with his head bowed. I really did try to keep the grin off my face and my giggle from escaping my lips, but it just wasn't happening.

"Lorena." I was pulled into the arms of Caius' mother as she neared.

"Mother." Cai greeted her with a smile and a kiss to the cheek.

"I heard that our Alpha couple had moved out of the pack house and immediately came to see what all the fuss..." She paused no doubt spotting the mate marks we were both proudly sporting.

The next second was pierced by a squeal as Lorena threw her arms around both of us pulling us in for a tight hug.

"When did this happen? It's only been a couple days since we talked, I didn't expect this so soon." The last part directed toward me. It would be a surprise to everyone. Especially with higher ranked wolves, it was custom to have a ceremony introducing new couples before they moved on to the next stage of the mating process.

When soulmates mates found each other they'd bond, but nothing was to progress until they'd been introduced to the pack as a couple. It was similar to how humans kept themselves pure until their wedding night.

Everyone would be in for a right shock.

"Would you like to come in?" I wasn't sure of what Cai had in the house to offer guests, hopefully there was something in. We'd need to go food shopping soon.

"No, no. I've got to head back to Phillip, we're heading out with some friends for lunch but I thought I'd quickly pop in." Her voice suddenly took a stern tone, "You know, it'd be nice if we heard from you once in a while. We are still your parents and we do love you very much."

"I can't speak for your son but you and Phillip are always welcome to drop by whenever you please."

"Oh, thank you, dear. And we will take you up on that. But I promise if the house is a rockin' we won't come a knockin.'" My face quickly flamed with heat as she came to the end of her sentence.

"Wouldn't wanna disrupt any grand-baby making." She giggled, turned and started back down the driveway. "See you both soon."

"Oh, my goddess." I muttered as Trent erupted with another jolt of laughter.

"Trent, go away!" I heard Cai order Trent while I avoided eye contact and moved into the house. Soon I felt Cai pressed against my back.

"How about I give you the grand tour," I nodded in reply before he gently took my hand and began to lead me around the house. Our new home.

CHAPTER THIRTEEN

W E WERE SAT IN THE kitchen as Cai started making us lunch. It was completely his idea; I did in no way ask but I did think it was a cute gesture. Until I found out that all we had in the cupboards were a few odd tins of soup.

"Chicken noodle or tomato?" Cai looked at me sheepishly from across the kitchen island.

"Tomato." As he moved around I couldn't keep my eyes off of him. I couldn't help but remember what he had looked like this morning, in bed, all ruffled and exposed. As the muscles of his back moved so did the t-shirt he was wearing. His tight jeans clung to his sculpted ass and his thick trunk like legs, I'm pretty sure they were the same jeans he'd worn the day I first met him. *They were rapidly becoming my favorite pair.*

"Do you wanna to have children?" I blurted as he turned back around to face me. I wasn't sure how this was better than being caught drooling over his body but I'd panicked.

"Yeah, of course. I'd love kids. Why? Because my mom mentioned it? Don't worry about that. There's no pressure." I smiled at his slight ramblings thinking it to be endearing.

"No. I've always wanted a big family. When we're ready of course." Although, as we talked about having children, I knew that I'd want to know more about our bond before ever committing to having children.

We still had no clue as to why or how we were bonded together and though we'd find out soon enough, I worried our bond would make it harder to conceive. Or worse still, the prophecy would have something to do with our offspring. It wouldn't have been the first time that had happened.

"How about we make a plan to go out? Just you and me, on a proper date."

"The last time we went out it wasn't an actual date so I'd be curious as to know how a 'proper' date with you, would go." As the laughing smile stretched across my face I flashback to the night we'd went out to the carnival. It seemed like so long ago and yet it had only been a week since.

Oh, how things could change in an instant.

We talked about the rogue situation around slurping up our soup. We decided we would deal with it tomorrow and just enjoy today, unpacking and spending as much time together as possible.

To divert my thoughts as Cai washed up, I inspected the design of the newly rebuilt kitchen. The benchtops were white adorned with chrome kitchen appliances, and the cabinets were light grey. There wasn't much color but I knew once we settled in we'd eventually get around to adding splashes of life here and there.

The inside of the house was gorgeous. It was very open planned, with oak flooring throughout except for the living room, study and all five bedrooms. If I'd had to design my own home I had no idea where I'd have even started, I thought Caius truly did an awesome job.

Plus, I loved the smile that lit up his face when he told me about all the changes and remodels he'd made just recently.

"We should go start unpacking." There was a twinkle in his eye as he stood looking at me, waiting for me to get up off my lazy ass. I sighed, this would probably take all afternoon.

As I entered the master bedroom, Cai close behind me, I couldn't help but pause and think of what a huge step this was. Boxes were stacked around the walls as I scanned the room. We were moving in together. I'd never lived with anyone aside from my parents, and so I'd never shared a room with anyone. I had a feeling this was going to be majorly awkward.

Where would I put my things? What side of the bed would I sleep on? Did he have a particular side?

I suppose it didn't matter much to me. I was a pretty much a starfish when it came to sleeping, I doubt him wanting the left side would change that. A little voice in my head let an evil laugh slip.

I turned to Caius who stood behind me. He was close, like really close. Personal bubble close. His raspy voice came out as just a breath against my skin, "I set your bags down in the closet."

"Thank you." My voice was only a whisper as the lack of space between us started to affect my mental capacity. Again.

The closet was already roughly divided into two, he'd already put away some of his things on the left side of the walk-in closet. I guessed I was to take the opposite side.

"I usually spread out in my sleep, will you be okay with that?" *He just had no idea how much I'd spread out. He he.* It had only taken me ten minutes to unpack everything from my bags but double that time to organize and reorganize everything. The radio had been playing softly from the bedroom mixed with the sounds of Cai moving around and shuffling boxes.

"Sure thing, I usually sleep on the right side. Will you be okay with that?" He called back as I rose from my spot on the ground in the closet. I walked to the door frame to silently watch as he flattened the cardboard boxes that had been, until half an hour ago, filled with his belongings.

As I watched on at his muscles working I knew he could sense my gaze on him. He never halted until all the boxes where flattened and leaning against the wall near the door.

The gorgeous man in front of me was the one I was going to share the rest of my life with, I didn't give a fuck what side of the bed was his and which was mine. He was mine, that was all that mattered. Finally finding some lady balls I strode across to Cai, pulled his face to me and captured his lips with mine.

I felt I'd never get used to the feeling that overtook me when our lips met. My whole body sizzled with heat and need and I pulled him even closer to my body.

I pushed us toward the bed not letting his lips escape from mine. We collapsed together onto the soft cushioning of the king bed. I pulled away first moving to repositioning onto my side. Facing him I traced every flawless feature with my eyes. His smile dulled slightly when he brushed his fingertips over the slight scar running down the side of my face.

I hoped it didn't bother him but even I couldn't see past the ugliness added to my face. Of course, I didn't have to look at it every two seconds, I went as far as avoiding reflective surfaces wherever possible. The scar wasn't massive and it was barely noticeable but I knew it was there. It only served to remind me of who put it there every time I seen it.

His hand dropped back to the bed in the space between us. "You're so beautiful."

My heart drummed a fast beat in my chest, I felt the rise in my pulse just about everywhere. Wetness began to pool in the corner of my eye. This sweet, gorgeous man was beyond what I had imagined as my mate. I felt so blessed and sent a silent promise to the Moon Goddess. I would spend forever cherishing this man, that I felt myself falling for.

))◐◑●◐◑((

"When you're ready, mom has been dying to have a big family dinner." Cai startled me from behind as he entered the kitchen. I had been lost in thought. It had been two days since we began to unpack our things in the new house. Everything was sorted except for Cai's office.

"Really?"

"Yeah, her and dad want to get to know you better. Plus, I thought it'd be a perfect opportunity for you to have your family and friends come to visit. I know last time they were here things were a bit rocky between us and I'd like for them to see that things have settled and that you're happy here."

"You are happy, right?" He looked so handsome standing there in light wash jeans and form fitting tee shirt that he distracted me. Although on anyone else I'm sure it wouldn't have looked so good or quite so tight. The slight furrow of his brow was what stung me. He didn't seem to know what he did to me, how he made me feel.

The nights we had spent together in this house were sweet, completely innocent, but special none the less. We had finally gone food shopping, we fought over the furniture placement; I felt the couch would be better on the other side of the living room, we had even started painting our very colorless bedroom.

I had also discovered just how limited Cai was as for what he could cook. Like actually, I had thought he'd been joking when he had said he wasn't skilled in the kitchen. So, feeling like a real suburban housewife I had taken over the cooking, but he would always sit in the kitchen, talking me through everything I did or helping whenever he could.

"I couldn't imagine being any happier, Caius… You've done that to me." And that was the truest statement that had ever passed through my lips.

I pecked his lips lovingly before turning back to stir the pasta sauce on the stove, "So when is this dinner taking place?"

"She suggested next Wednesday night if that's okay?"

"Okay, I'll make a call. Any preferences as to what I make for dinner?"

"Nope, it's all up to you." Of course, he'd eat whatever was put in front of him he wouldn't care what it was.

Until all Caius' things had been moved over he was still having to go to work at his old office. And, since the rogue attack a few days ago he had been extra busy so when I woke in the mornings he was gone, not usually arriving back home until tea time. But I cherished every sparse moment I got to spend with him, even if it was just the very mundane task of making dinner together and enjoying our evening meals chatting away.

"We're having Cai's parents over for dinner on Wednesday night. We wanted to ask if you'd join our little dinner party?" I spoke to my aunt over the phone on Monday morning.

"Of course dear, that sounds like a great idea. I can't wait to see you, see how things are going. Plus, it'd be so great to catch up with Lorena and Phillip. What time should we be there?"

I spent the next half hour on the phone, you'd have thought we hadn't spoken for years. There just always seemed to be something else to talk about. I was thrilled to hear that few of my old pack mates had found their soulmates mates over in my aunts' pack. It reminded me that there were friends here in Cai's pack that I should check in with.

Soon. I thought to myself as hung up with my aunt only to dial the number she gave me for Carson's mobile. I had been meaning to keep in contact with both her and Dante but it had been a busy weekend with Cai.

My phone call to Carson had only been brief because she was getting ready for warrior training, which I congratulated her on. After walking away from the landline, I felt the loneliness set in again. Huffing out I turned and headed upstairs, I was sick of this and from that moment forward I vowed to keep myself busy. So, for hours I occupied my time by using the leftover light grey paint from our bedroom to paint all the interior doors of the house. As well as wanting to keep myself active, I also wanted some color to break up the whiteness of the interior walls.

I missed him. I knew that he had work to do, no one could understand that more than I did. But that didn't keep away the coldness that attacked me when I wasn't with him. I smiled at how far I'd come and at how much my life had returned to a somewhat normal state. I wasn't a social butterfly but I'd always had someone right around the corner to talk to and lately that had been Cai.

Thinking about him wasn't enough. I decided it was time for a break from staring at the crappy daytime programmes on the telly so I made my way to the kitchen. It was about lunch time, *maybe I could bring Cai lunch? I had to go out anyway.*

Despite picking up a few bits and bobs at the shops over the weekend there wasn't anything too extravagant in; we'd been living off of sandwiches, pasta and cereal. It wasn't fancy but I decided on ham and cheese sandwiches, I just really only needed an excuse to see Cai at work.

"The house is so big and empty without you. I was getting restless, so I thought I'd pop in then maybe I'd see if Mia was around." I felt the need to be doing something, I had a feeling hanging out with Mia and Sophie would be a breath of fresh air.

"Usually I'd have something here you could help me with but there's nothing for you to do. I'm sorry Kira. And, did you mean Mia White?"

"Yeah, we met a little while ago. She seemed nice." It'd

been a while since I last spoke to her, I hoped she was still good for going to lunch sometime this week.

"Okay, well I'm glad you're getting comfortable with the pack." He smiled flashing me his pearly whites.

"Maybe I could start joining in on pack training?" I knew it would be different, attending training sessions with other members of the pack, in a new pack and in beast form none the less, but I was ready to put my body back to work. Once upon a time I had really enjoyed pack training, I was excited to go pack to it.

"We train combat in ranking groups but general fitness we do all together. You're welcome to tag along with me anytime you'd like, I'll let you know when the next one is. Though, beware that I'll be stuck to your side like fucking superglue." He warned but I smiled wickedly at the invitation of having him by my side for hours on end.

I left his office with a kiss before going off in search of Mia. After wandering the house and the gardens disappointed at not finding her I walked to the path that led through the trees and to the main village street.

I picked out a full load of groceries having no idea what I was actually going to make for tonight's dinner party, along with some tins of sunshine yellow wall paint, *another little project to keep me busy.*

Trying to juggle everything outside of the store called 'Big Al's Superstore' I spotted Trent across the street. We had a bit of a weird, hot and cold, let's say 'friendship' but I didn't hate him. He was irritating as hell but he was Cai's Beta for a reason and I trusted Cai's judgement.

"Trent!" I called to him as he walked closely with two other guys. His eyes caught mine and I waved both arms frantically, my grin instantaneous. Him and his companions walked across the road to where I had dumped all my bags on the sidewalk pavement.

"Alpha-Luna. It's so good to finally meet you." One of the guys with Trent spoke somewhat nervously. I hadn't been introduced to either of the guys before and I was sure I hadn't seen them around either.

"You too…" I shook his outstretched hand as I studied him. He had curly ginger hair and was probably only a few inches taller than me. The glee on his face resembled that of a kid in a toy store and I couldn't believe I'd done that to someone.

"Oh, I'm Simon. I'm a warrior here in Night."

"And this is my older brother, Tommy." Trent said. I could see the resemblance between Trent and his brother as Tommy stepped forward. Tommy's laugh lines were more prominent, his hair was longer and his eyes seemed lighter than Trent's, in color and in a way I couldn't name. Happier, I suppose.

"Where are you guys heading? Are you out on serious pack business?" I smiled after nodding a hello to Tommy.

"No, just grabbing coffee. What are you doing out?" My eyes narrowed at Trent, he made it sound like I wasn't allowed out of my cage. *Ooh I'd so love the chance to hit him, knock him off his high horse.*

"Are you guys heading back to the pack house anytime soon?" Completely ignoring Trenton, I spoke to Tommy and Simon laying my charming smile on thick. My eyes flicked down to the bags and paint cans at my feet, making sure nothing had fallen over.

"Yeah, we're heading back now. Where are you on your way to? Did you need a hand with those bags?" Simon was already reaching out and picking four of the carrier bags up off the ground.

"Awe, that's so sweet of you. I was actually just going back to Cai." Tommy then bent and plucked up the cans of paint for me.

"Thanks. So, what have you guys been up to today?" I lifted the last carrier bag into my arms before we started walking up the street, leaving a scowling Trent to follow behind.

"My mate, Irene and I have been at the playground with our daughter. Trent came out of the house going on the hunt for a chocolate chip muffin. As soon as he mentioned it, Irene pushed me along to bring one back for her." Tommy laughed, the twinkle in his eyes now explaining itself. He was in love.

"You appear to be muffin-less?" I giggled as I inspected him, he hadn't been carrying anything of his own.

"The bakery makes everything fresh daily but they do different flavors and types of cakes every day. No chocolate chip muffins today." I smiled at his forlorn voice, he'd be in trouble when he got back.

"And what about you Simon?" I turned to my left directing my attention onto him.

"I've been holed up in the entertainment room with some buddies playing on the Xbox. I needed some fresh air, they're not the nicest smelling bunch." His laugh was as loud as it was startling, making it to the end of the street and turning the corner.

"Tell me about your daughter, it's hard to imagine Trent as an uncle." I turned back to Tommy walking to my right, I was sure Trent grumbled under his breath at my dig.

"I know, right? Little Annie is nearly four. Absolute light of my life, but we're really excited to be having another pup." We arrived to the peak of the slight hill continuing on the path through the blooming trees.

"Your mate's pregnant?" He nodded his head with a grin. "How far along? Do you guys know what you're having yet?"

"She's six months pregnant with a baby boy." I bet he was super happy about that, wasn't it every guys dream to have a boy to kick a football around with? Not that you could complain either way.

"Awe, that's so sweet. You guys must be ecstatic; I can't wait get started on our family. I'm sorry to say, but I have a feeling ours are going to be just spoilt." A wistful thought of our future flitted through my mind. *One day.*

"They all are," He wrapped his arms fondly around the tall heavily pregnant blonde that had just approached us. We all stopped as he introduced me to Irene, the lovely lady in front of me. She was very sweet and even tried to get her daughters attention to say hello. She proudly pointed out the little blonde girl on the jungle gym surrounded by all the other pack kids. She was a beauty just like her mother.

With Simon and Trent, I quickly left them outside, I felt I was intruding on their private family time but promised I'd happily see them around. Trent huffed and puffed all the way inside the house and up to Cai's office about having to carry my paint.

"Honey, I'm home." I called as I led my little helpers into my mates' office. He was leaning back in his chair looking suspiciously trouble free.

"It was nice meeting you, Alpha-Luna." He stumbled

as he set down my bags next to the guest chair, where I'd taken up residence.

"You too, Simon." I waved goodbye as he walked out the open door.

"What time is it?" I asked, noting Trent hadn't yet left the room.

"Trent, what have you got plans tonight?" After moments of silence and only a raised eyebrow as an answer, I went on to elaborate. "We're having people over for dinner, would you like to join us?"

It was silent again but this time his eyes flickered to Caius. Examining Cai closer I realized they looked to be communicating with their eyes. My eyes went back and forth between them wishing I knew what was being said. Their power struggle seemed to end when Trent released a heavy sigh. "Fine."

Despite how we acted towards each other, I didn't hate Trent. I could strangle his attitude but he was Caius' best friend and I respected that. I liked to think that one day I'd soften him up enough so that his shell would crack and he wouldn't be such a hardass all the time. I knew he was unmated and I softly suspected that maybe he needed a lady in his life.

"Goody. Come by for about six." I smiled politely making him turn and stalk out the office. I looked to Cai expectantly across his desk.

"He'll be there." Caius' happy grin and nonchalant automatically made me roll my eyes.

"It's nearly three o'clock and I'm done for the day. Let's go home." We returned home via Caius' smoking red Spider, all of my shopping safely tucked away in the boot.

CHAPTER FOURTEEN

STUMBLING INTO THE KITCHEN, WE began pouring out the shopping I'd bought onto the countertops. From sorting through the groceries, I decided I would make a big batch of lasagna saddled with roasted vegetables. I'd also make potato salad while serving a cheeky store bought apple pie for desert. *I was good, but I wasn't that good. Homemade apple pie just took more effort than I had in me right now.*

"Go get ready, I'll set the table." Cai said as he finished wiping down the kitchen benches. Everything was set; the lasagna was waiting to join the roast vegetables in the oven, the potato salad and brownie mixture was sitting in the fridge. I was a mess. I would definitely need a quick shower before our guests arrived.

I was excited, I wanted to show Caius off to my family plus this had all the trimmings of being a great night. I thought it was a nice idea to have everyone we loved over to meet and I was thankful to Lorena for suggesting it. I'd also been meaning to ask Lorena about helping me plan the Luna ceremony, hopefully I'd get a chance to talk to her about it tonight.

I had only just finished smoothing on my summery, black floral printed dress when there was a heavy thudding at the front door. *They were here.*

"I'll get the door." Caius called up the stairs as I slipped into some black flats. Passing the mirror, I liked the bright happiness shining from the eyes of the young woman that looked back at me. I raced down to the kitchen putting the lasagna in the oven as Cai welcomed people into the house. As our guests slowly started to trickle in I was pleasantly surprised to see Dante, Noah, Katherine and Andrew trail in amongst my family. I didn't realize until I saw them all together standing in the kitchen doorway how much I had missed them, these people that had always been there for me.

"Don't worry, we brought extra food!" Noah announced with a hearty chuckle gaining laughs from some of the others. I said my greetings while giving out a round of hugs before I moved to serving drinks. I watched from the kitchen as my family started migrating into the dining room. The grin on my face couldn't be contained as Caius introduced his parents to my hometown friends, Lorena and Aunt Mary hugging like long lost teen BFF's.

Caius laid out extra place settings for our unexpected guests, my eyes glued to him and his every rippling movement. He was so close to perfect it was intimidating at times. My mind caught on comparing him and our life, for the first real time, to Asher and the very different path I would've been on. I didn't want to imagine my life any other way, I wouldn't have traded it or Caius for anything.

Everyone started to take their seats just as Trent strolled into the kitchen and I took that as my queue to bring out the bread rolls, potato salad and the salad that I'm sure Katherine made. I took my seat opposite Cai on the end of the long mahogany table. Though the table was big we still struggled to all fit in, having to bunch up for more room. Seated to my left was Dante and on my right, was Lorena with all of the men sat toward Cai's end of the table.

Lorena, Aunt Mary and Katherine were discussing Caius and myself and while my ears burned slightly to be a part of that conversation I was directing my attention to Lily as I asked her about her mate. As I looked around the table I could've only wished my parents had been there to join in the festivities, they would've loved it.

"I'm going to go check on dinner." I said to no one in particular, then looked to Dante who I hadn't even had the chance to say a proper hello to. "Dante, wanna come help?"

I smirked slightly as I got up remembering all the times before that Dante, Carson and I had snuck off to gossip about boys, trash talk about our parents and bitch about the cheerleaders. The roasting vegetables weren't quite ready but I pulled out the lasagna from the oven before turning my full attention to my long-time friend. I wrapped my arms tightly around her having missed her so.

"What's been happening while I've been gone?" I asked as we pulled away and Dante went on to tell me the latest news.

"Well, I started working at the bakery in Shadow last week. Carson and Tyler are still going strong; Alpha Liam has been good to them. To everyone in the pack, really. We've practically resumed our lives in similar spots we were in before... before everything happened." Our silence as we both thought about that 'everything' was all-consuming.

"How about you? Have you found your mate? I thought there'd be a good chance he might've been in Shadow." I said, hoping for a quick diversion for my mind.

"Nope, still nothing on that front. But, you never know, he could be just right around the corner." Her smile was optimistic and for that I was glad, I didn't want her to give up on finding her Mr. Right. I could only pray she didn't have to wait too much longer.

"I see you've been claimed." It took me a full minute and her pointing at my neck for me to catch on to what she'd meant. "How does it feel? Does he make you happy?"

I nodded, sighing out heavily in contentment. My smile grew as I spoke the honest to Goddess truth, "It's amazing. He's amazing, like beyond anything I ever imagined."

"I'm so happy for you Kira, you deserve to be happy." She hugged me tight and I relished that I was finally on the path to my happily ever after.

We brought dinner through to our hungry patrons and laughed at everyone's hooting and hollering. We were certainly a loud bunch, luckily we didn't have any close neighbors.

"If you'll excuse me," I said a while later, avoiding Caius' eye I quickly made my way to the downstairs bathroom. Dinner had been going great and I was thrilled that everyone seemed to like my cooking. My mother was an amazing cook and tonight I had wanted to make her proud; she taught me everything I knew about the kitchen.

It was shortly after starting our main course when I'd

started to feel clammy. At first I worried it was the food but everyone else seemed to be fine. My head was pounding and although I loved all the happy noise and chatter, I felt like I was going to explode.

Once secured behind the closed door I ran the tap as cold as I could and started pressing my wet hands to my face and neck. It was really warm tonight; I was sweating bullets. Sagging against the cool bathroom tile, I caught my breath. I knew if I weren't so concerned with cooling myself down I'd be running around trying to find the thermostat.

Cupping my hands, I brought them up drinking down the cool liquid. The relief the cold water sliding down my throat brought had only lasted a few minutes before the blazing heat set in again. Knowing I'd have to return to the dinner table I patted myself down, lucky that I had decided not to wear much make-up. No one wants to see running mascara and smudged lip gloss.

Opening the door, the scent wafted over me so intensely I stumbled, only catching myself by holding onto the door frame. From here I could see Caius stood at the other end of the hallway. We stood frozen drinking each other in. In his presence, I felt myself cooling down slightly, he was the ice water raining over my burning fire.

"Kira, your scent...you're going into heat." He exclaimed, his eyes becoming wild with the thought.

Oh, fuck!

I rushed back into the bathroom as I heard Caius rushing about, dismissing our dinner guests. Although I felt bad for cutting the night short and essentially kicking everyone out, I knew the sooner we were alone the better.

A Lycan-wolfs heat is just another perk of being a

female. We're taught at a young age that soon after meeting and marking your mate females experience 'heat' to hurry along sex. This therefore seals the bond between mates. Luckily it's a once in a lifetime kind of thing but the effect it has is that of tidal wave which lasts about a week.

During hell week, the female experiences most of it, starting with the change in her scent then her body fevering and flaming. Both males and females are subject to having a heightened sexual appetite and a primitive longing of closeness.

The front door slammed closed with a loud thump before Cai appeared in the doorway. He carried my aching body up the stairs silently while dread slowly began filling every inch of my being. I had expected this, no she-wolf is lucky enough to escape the wrath of this bitch. But, Cai and I hadn't exactly had the 'talk' yet. Not the sex talk, obviously, we knew how that went, but the 'our future' talk.

I was gently set on our mattress before Caius went about getting ready for bed. I shivered rapidly wishing I had more layers on top of my dress. "Cai?"

He paused across the room, shirtless and in the process of putting our shoes away and he called back to me. "Kira?"

I felt his eyes on me as he stalked closer towards me, when he finally stopped in front of me I couldn't ignore his gaze anymore. His rough hands swept gently along my cheek, caressing it. The intense hunger that lit his eyes made my skin prickle. Enraptured by his gaze I leaned up, sliding my hands along his smooth naked flesh. Gripping his shoulders tightly I tugged him forward, wanting him to be within close range.

LUNAR ACCORD

My lips brushed against his in a soft kiss, I swear it started off innocent but before long my itch for him grew. I pulled away for a quick breath and he took advantage of the opportunity by pushing me back onto the bed. As he crawled on top of my body his lips pressed hot kisses up my body. My legs fell open as he settled himself above me, his lips resuming their insistent admiration of mine. My nails dug into the skin of his back as his tongue forced its way into my mouth.

While one hand held his body weight up the other took to the exploration of my body. A groan erupted from the back of Caius' throat and I felt it reverberate through me. We both took great pleasure as my every curve was over turned and thoroughly attended to. Through my dress I could feel the blazing trail his hand and long steady fingers wove.

Becoming too overwhelmed by the passion, I pulled back. Caius continued to pepper kisses along my neck, lingering over the sensitive mark I bore there. With my breathing harbored I tried to get the words out. I wanted to tell him that we needed to stop before things got out of hand but the words were caught in my thought, overpowered by my moaning.

"Cai," My voice was weak, just that of a whisper. I tried again hoping for more conviction in my tone, "Caius."

He pulled back with our eyes locked on each other. I could see part of my reflection in his glassy grey eyes. I just had to be honest with him, I couldn't let this continue. "I don't know if I'm ready, and I don't want this to be forced on us Cai. I want it to be our choice when we have sex for the first time, and when we have children I want it to have been on our timing, not because we were too horny to control ourselves."

I huffed out a powerful breath. I hated this. I wanted, desperately, to be intimate with Caius but that would have to wait for now. With the heat causing such an increased chance of pregnancy, I wouldn't risk it. I wanted a family but it wasn't something to rush into, especially without even having had a proper conversation about it.

"I understand." He sighed, as he rolled himself off me and positioned himself by my side. "It's something we haven't talked about but whenever you're ready, I'm here waiting. To talk about it, I mean."

I smiled softly at the tenderness my mate offered me. My eyelids started to droop closed weighing heavily with tiredness and exhaustion. Cai shifted and took my hand before whispering, "Get some sleep, love."

I squeezed his hand in mine as I held it close to my heart. *Goodnight my prince.*

I rumbled from my deep sleep to Caius' shifting beside me but was quickly pulled back into the shadows of slumber. When I fully gained consciousness, it was past nine and I realized I had missed Caius' and my morning run. That had become our routine in the mornings before breakfast. By this time, he would've usually already been out of the house.

Suddenly saddened by the thought that I had missed him, I moved from the bed to the bathroom. I was clammy from experiencing the full force of my heat during the night and a calming bath sounded like heaven. Much like a period, the first days were usually the worst. I could only hope last nights' intense burning was the brunt of it.

194

LUNAR ACCORD

The bath cooled my body and left me feeling deeply refreshed. I dressed in shorts and a tank top after assuming I wouldn't be leaving the house anytime soon. Over the next week I would be confined to the house and only a select few people. My scent had changed to become more appealing to males, not just Cai but all male Lycans would be affected.

Caius had been waiting in the kitchen with breakfast already on the stove when I wondered downstairs. His scent almost knocked me sideways as I entered through the archway to the kitchen, his scent was potent, he had been here a while. "Good morning."

I sighed in complete wonder at the man I could call mine. I smiled to myself at the fact that he had stayed home just to be with me.

That day we kept ourselves occupied with the distraction that board games and movies brought. I promised myself after last nights' slip up that I'd be careful to put distance between us.

As I had anticipated I had been house bound, with Cai, for the past four days. Considering the comedown in the intensity of my heat I assumed I wouldn't have had long left before it was all over. Today would've been the first day I'd seen anyone aside from Caius. He had been good to me, taking care of me but also making sure we never overstepped our boundaries. It had been hard, to stay away from him and all my desires, with all the hormones rushing around my body drawing me closer to him, tempting me to cross that line.

Lorena's visit today would put some much-needed breathing space between me and her son, for a few hours anyway. We spent our time wisely going over all the details of our mating ceremony that was to be held on the upcoming Friday. She insisted that we had to invite all our allied packs but it was my idea to send an invite to The Elders up in Canada. With our short amount of time together having been so hectic I'd nearly forgotten all about our underlying situation. The big question mark that was our "prophecy" still needed to be answered, and Caius had seemed sure it'd be The Elders that held the answers.

It couldn't do any harm to invite them, they probably wouldn't travel so far from home but if they did it would save us the trip. It was also a given that my family and my friends be there. Then there was going over my preferences for music and food and such. It was almost like a wedding reception but I didn't have any preferences, Lorena's face lit when I told her she had complete control. I quickly grew wary of her giddiness and hoped I had made the right decision.

Monday, after a long week cooped up and my heat finally over, Cai and I decided it would be nice to get some fresh air. With some persistent begging on my part Caius finally agreed for us to oversee the pack's weekly training that was taking place. We strolled over to the training grounds, I lapped up the soft wind brushing through my hair as Cai led the way.

Out in an open grassy field there were crowds of people. I would've went so far as to say there could've been hundreds. I stood back in awe at the number of people gathered in one place, all at the same time. I knew packs grew their numbers up into the thousands range but back in my old pack we were only tiny compared to that.

This would've been my first official appearance as the

Alphas mate; I was shaking like a leaf. To have so many eyes on me, judging me solely on what rumors they'd heard, was nerve-wrecking.

I hoped that I would find Mia today at the pack training session after Caius said that the children were watched over nearby. I didn't have any friends here and she was the only person that I had genuinely liked.

Cai squeezed my hand reassuring me that with him by my side we'd tackle the crowd together. People parted, bowed their head and offered congratulations as we walked towards Trent and a few others who stood seemingly at the front of them all. So far so good, my nervousness lessened.

Caius and I stood back as Trent began to lead the Lycans in their weekly fitness training session. He started with a warm up then moved onto defense and offensive attacks. It was all pretty basic but it was definitely something I had missed being involved in. Even as a kid training together as a pack was a big part of my life, and who I am.

Looking at each individual pack member there were only a dozen or so of whom I recognized. Mia's brunette haired head being one of them. A few caught my watchful eye for different reasons, the prison guard Cregg being one of them. The others were women that gave me looks of over the top interest. *What the hell were they so interested in?*

Drawing to a break, chatter began to erupt amongst the pack wolves. Some were star-fished on the ground with exhaustion, some showering themselves with their water bottles. A couple from the front row came up to grab our attention. The woman had cropped red hair and was probably around my age while the guy had dark hair paired with pale skin and bright green eyes; they were a stunning pair.

"Alpha. Luna." They both bowed their head in respect after stopping before us.

"Kira you might recognize Oliver, my Gamma. And this is his mate Keri-Ann, one of our Deltas."

"Right. It's lovely to meet you both." I smiled politely back at them, I admit I had seen Oliver around but I hadn't thought of him as Gamma material from his appearance. Oliver was tall but was scrawny looking. I felt awful having judged him on his appearance and mentally prayed forgiveness for my oversight.

Caius' growl thundered beside me pulling me from my thoughts and back into the moment. I hadn't even realized I'd zoned out. I felt, rather than heard, the silence that fell upon everyone surrounding us. I looked to Cai wondering what had caused him to become this upset, but the murderous look on his face told me nothing.

"I'm so sorry Alpha. I meant no disrespect, I was only saying that I was glad those types of things don't occur nowadays." Keri-Ann spoke trying to calm the Alpha, panic rapidly beginning to fill her eyes.

"What was that? I didn't hear what you said." I sent her a small smile trying to lure her into repeating what had just upset Cai.

She sighed before softly repeating, "I was just saying that you'd have a few challengers if this had been back in the olden days. But I'm glad that won't be the case. I wish no harm upon the new Luna of Night." She bowed her head before kneeling of the ground at my feet.

"What the heck?" I exclaimed in a complete state of

shock. Quickly I gripped her arm and pulled her up back onto her feet. "What did you mean? Challengers?"

She looked to Cai in a frazzled state and then back to me. "I'm so sorry Luna."

"You two should get back to training, I'm sure I'll see you around." I dismissed them as Trent began to round up the group to continue on with his lesson.

Squaring my shoulders and straightening my spine I turned to Caius. I wanted an answer and I would damn well get one. "Caius, what did she mean?"

"Once upon a time, after males found their mate sometimes there'd be women who felt superior and felt the need to challenge their new Luna. So, they would fight over the title. Whomever won would stay and become the Alphas mate, the loser would be exiled from the pack." He sighed and upon closer examination his face was contorted into a grimace.

"That's something they left out of the history books." I had never heard of such a thing. Although it was believable of our Elders, I wondered if it ever happened in amongst my family. My dad had never mentioned anything of the sort either because he hadn't known anything of it or because it was something he had wanted hidden from me.

"I'm sorry that I got upset." Caius apologized while his eyes fell to the ground.

"It's okay, but if it makes you feel any better, I would accept any challenge and I'd kick ass too." I semi joked. Pulling him close enough to wrap my arms around his neck I leaned up to peck his lips. "I would fight for you, Cai."

A hush fell around us, the large crowd suddenly silent. Again. Turning to see what had caused the change in atmosphere this time, I caught Trent's eye. He was stock still with eyes worried and wired open looking straight through me. Perusing the crowd, I saw all eyes had turned to one woman stood amongst them.

"I repeat, I challenge the Alphas mate for the Luna title." There were gasps of shock and cries of dismay from the people surrounding the blonde haired she-wolf.

My ears rung as I looked back to Trent, feeling Caius' low growl from behind me in my bones. *Was she for real?*

In my position, I would've thought I'd have possessed more rage by being challenged, most Alpha wolves would've. In reality, I was outraged but more over I was amused. The woman wasn't someone I had encountered before and although taller than me she didn't seem to have any other advantage. She was an ordinary Lycan, what did she expect the outcome to be of going up against an Alpha. I could've only seen the battle ending in bloodshed, her bloodshed. I'd have to try extra hard to restrain my inner beasts' natural instincts.

"I accept." My voice being the sound of a pin dropping as it rang out across the field. With my back straight I looked to Trent once again and nodded softly.

CHAPTER FIFTEEN

CAI'S ARMS SLITHERED AROUND MY belly and pulled me back against his body. He was shaking, I didn't know if it was out of anger or nervousness. His head burrowed into the side of my neck. I felt his deep breathing, his chest expanding and deflating against my back. As he released a long breath into my neck I felt the fine hairs on my arms stand on end, a sudden shiver running through me.

"You don't have to do this. She should be exiled, or worse, for even mentioning such a thing." His voice, low and gravelly, was the sexiest thing I had ever heard and even caused a clenching between my thighs that astounded me; we were in public after all. After reprimanding my body and recovering from my shock I turned in his arms to face him.

"I agree completely. But, you can hand out your punishments *after* I make a fool out of her."

"No one will ever take my place by your side Caius," I said it to reassure him but it was more of a promise than a statement. And it was possibly the truest thing I had ever said.

"Nor mine." He kissed my lips with such passion, such fervor, that my mind flashed back to the first night of my heat. It had been so nice to give in to the ecstasy that plagued my entire being. I pulled away quickly putting an end to what could've easily turned into a free show for the people around us. *To be continued…soon, my love.*

"Who is she?" I asked Caius as we waited for Trent to set up the match.

"Her name is Reagan Hollick, she's an unranked pack wolf."

"And do you have any idea as to why she's challenged me?" My head tilted, eyebrow raised and eyes narrowing only caused him to let out a loud booming chuckle.

"No. Honestly, I don't. I've never had much interaction with her, at all, so I don't know her very well."

"Then, she's just a snobby bitch that wants the title and thinks she's better than everyone else." I muttered as Trent signaled that it was time.

I was soon stood across from the blonde woman inside of a marked out, grassy makeshift ring. Cai's pack members stood around to form a human wall, caging us in with their excitement to see the fight. Most of them weren't happy about their Alphas mate being challenged by one of their own but there were still a few anxious to see how I'd handle myself.

These people had never met an Alpha Female before, let alone seen one in a fight. They were morbidly curious to see me in action which in a way I could understand. I'm sure I would've been interested to see the showdown just as much.

My father had tried to shelter me from pondering eyes

all of my life. He'd guarded me from exactly this, not wanting the pressure of people's expectations or judgements weighing on my shoulders.

The first few minutes waiting in the ring no words were spoken, I still didn't know a thing about her or why we were battling it out physically. I could feel the Lycans rage in my body, building and starting to seep over into my human body. With Alpha dominated blood running through my veins We did not like to be challenged.

I wouldn't be as strong or as agile as normal, my training had been severely lacking, so I chose to use a more tactful approach by playing defense. But as Trent read out the short list of rules and started us off, I was confident that it would be an easy match.

My right leg moved back slightly to give me more balance, my hands curled into fists moving high to defend myself. Reagan took on a similar stance and started to bounce on her feet. She looked like a wind-up toy ready to spring into action. I was ready for her.

She moved forward and we started to circle each other. I wanted to see if she had any weaknesses I could visibly point out. Quickly peaking my interest was how heavily she guarded her face, leaving her ribs and body nearly completely open for attack. She lunged forward, I side stepped her and watched as she missed wildly. She tried again to get close to me and I let her, she extended her arm for a few harmless jabs. She kicked out her leg aiming high, I grabbed her ankle and threw her leg away from me causing her to stumble.

I pulled back my arm and launched my fist in for a knockout right hook. My hand connected with her jaw and she fell to the ground instantaneously, she hadn't seen it coming. I jumped on top of her quickly to keep her pinned to the ground with my body weight. This fight was won upon knock out or tap out. I really hoped I wasn't going to have to pummel her from this position to win.

I gripped her wrists with my hands to pin them down. "Surrender?"

"No." She gritted out, wiggling and bucking wildly. She managed to throw me off using her hips, reversing our roles. She straight-shooted punch after punch to my face, most of which I managed to block with my arms.

With one of her punches causing my hand to bang against my mouth and as the blood leaked into my mouth, the copper taste lingering on my tongue. I decided that enough was enough. Playtime was over, the bitch had busted my lip. Still blocking her feeble strikes with one arm, the other reared back and powered into her stomach. As she arched over me my other hand took grip of her neck.

I flipped us and squeezed my thighs around her torso my hand still on her neck. As her hands went up the clawed at mine my pressure only increased. "Surrender!"

I was met with silence as her eyes wildly looked for an escape and her body wriggled under the pressure. Her head bobbled, rubbing her already dirty hair further into the dirt and grass.

I slowly released my grip on her neck and stood upright above her. I kept my eyes on her the whole time only stepping back when two guards hauled her ass up off the ground at Trent's' command. Caius was quickly by my side as the crowd around us cheered at my victory.

"I think I've had enough fresh air for today. Can we go home now?" I turned to Cai and said. His response was a throaty chuckle and a nod. We made our way in the direction of home leaving people to chatter and disperse in our wake.

We arrived home to Lorena in the kitchen, cooking up a storm. As soon as she saw me she had demanded to know what'd happened. She'd been furious when we'd told her that I'd been challenged by one of our pack members. After giving me a tight hug she sent me away to bathe and clean myself up before dinner. By the stink eye she'd been giving Cai I could only assume he was about to get a verbal thrashing.

It had been a week since the fight. I hadn't left the house much after that, except to run errands with Caius. The week had passed by quickly as I started counting down the days until our mating ceremony.

Knocking at my door caused me to I flutter to the mirror to check my appearance one last time. It was time, this was it.

I'd woken up this morning in bed with Caius, excitement bubbling in my stomach before quickly being pulled away by Lorena. She had spent nearly the whole day with me. We had gone out to eat, we'd gotten our hair done at the local salon and then spent the rest of the day prepping for tonight.

Apparently, she hadn't wanted Caius to see me while I was getting ready so she had my guest room cleaned and stocked with everything I could've possibly needed to get myself ready for the ceremony. The amount of makeup and beauty supplies could've prepped a room full of pageant queens for a month, I'd barely made a dent in any of it.

"Kira, are you ready? It's time." His voice reverberated through the solid wood door, the only thing that was separating us. My insides melted at the very sound of Caius' voice. We hadn't even been apart a full twelve hours and yet, it had felt like a year since I'd seen him.

My reflection made me sigh dreamily. Lorena had done a great job at helping me pick out a dress. I thought the royal red coloring was elegant without the dress being too over the top extravagant. The neckline was low enough to show off my assets without being inappropriate. The dress was fitted around my chest and had lace three quarter sleeves. It tapered out slightly at my waist, flowing down to my knees.

"Come in." I answered, terrified and on edge of his reaction to my, very different, appearance. I wasn't the type to get made up very often and Cai was yet to see me this way.

The door knob twisted slowly and the door pushed away from its frame then he emerged through the opening.

"Kira…" His eyes wide and his smile sweet, he eyed at me from head to toe. "You look absolutely stunning. There aren't words to describe how utterly breathtaking you look."

Like a hunter stalking his prey he moved towards me. He leaned down toward me, his lips only a breath away from mine. My arms much like snakes that seek warmth wrapped themselves around his neck pulling myself up to properly greet him. Fireworks blasted off in my head as his tongue darted into my mouth giving me a taste of him. A taste I'd grown to love and predominantly crave.

I opened my mouth wider as my chest rubbed against

his, his erection hardening against my belly. His large hands gripped my waist, the heat burning through my dress. He let out a pained groan while pulling his lips away but resting his forehead on mine.

"You'll be the death of me. The festivities haven't even started yet and I already can't wait for this night to be over. I just want you all to myself."

My heart soared at his sweet words. His tenderness still surprised me, even after all the time we had spent together. I'd never felt so loved or cherished in all my life, he'd made me feel things that I had never thought were possible.

"My father and Trent are waiting in the office for us." *Right...* The formal part of the ceremony awaited us. He led me to the office located in the pack house where indeed his father and Trent were seated and waiting on us. Upon entering I noticed the way the room was a lot less cluttered, I hadn't seen it since Caius moved all of his work home with him.

We all said quick greetings before taking a seat and getting on with the main part of the night. While the celebration took place tonight, this was the part that mattered. This would be where I got officially sworn into Caius' pack, the Night pack. I would be introduced later tonight as Alpha Female of the Night pack, that's when the festivities would begin. It was still a chilling thought; I'd never been in any other pack then my own and never thought I would be either.

"Kira Brookes, do you swear your allegiance and loyalty to the Night pack?" Phillip, Cai's father, started the ritualistic vows. To which I eagerly replied yes.

"Your love and faith to Caius Killian Matthews?" Looking directly into Cai's eyes, I replied a firm yes.

"Do you swear to protect our sacred land and its people to the best of your abilities?" He asked.

"On my life, yes." I answered his last question.

I found myself on edge as I listened to Phillip repeat his part to Caius. But, as I knew he would, my Cai took the questions in his stride.

After all was said and signed, with Trent to witness, we followed Phillip as he led the way to the after party. I felt slightly light headed and was glad the packs didn't practice blood oaths anymore. Someone poking at me with a needle to take blood would not have helped my case in that moment in time.

"Introducing Alpha Caius Matthews and his new mate, Alpha Female Kira Brookes." Phillip announced as he wheeled out onto the back patio of the pack house.

My cheeks were flaming red hot, but Caius grabbed my hand and pulled me out through the back doors before I could think to turn back. I was temporarily stunned at the sight that greeted me. The field had been transformed with lights, color splashed everywhere and people filling every inch of space.

"So? What do you think dear? Do you like it?" Lorena rushed up to me all smiles while bouncing around like a toddler. That woman and her enthusiasm for life and everything it contained was something I admired greatly.

My eyes flickered around the garden. I understood then why she had wanted the celebration at night. Fairy lights hung everywhere the eye could see, from tree to tree and from post to post, they outshined the moon.

"Lorena, it's gorgeous." I said as my eyes continued to take everything in.

"Yeah mom, you've really outdone yourself." He said pulling her into a hug.

"You're welcome my dears. Now, I'll leave you two to mingle. Your father and I will catch up with you both later." I smiled after her as she walked over to Phillip who was off talking to an older pair.

"Kira, this is Alpha John and his mate, Sabrina. They're our neighbors from the Moon pack." He spoke about the middle-aged couple that had captured our attention. The man, John, looked to be a few years younger than my uncle. He had brown hair that was slightly greying at the temples. He stood tall and proud as his mate stood under his arm looking stunning in a dark blue skater style dress.

"Hello, thank you for coming. It's lovely to meet you both." I say graciously as we start our evening off.

"We've longed to meet you. It's such a pleasure." Sabrina said as she took my hand, shaking it gently. I was flattered.

As it turned out a lot of allied Alphas and packs were invited to come join our festivities. Alpha John and Sabrina were only the first of the seemingly millions of people I was introduced to.

"Do they all know?" I asked Caius as we found a moment alone to get ourselves a drink.

"They know the simplified version. That I'm mated to the Alpha Female, that's it." A small smirk made an appearance on his lips at his own words. He was proud of my Alpha status and wanted to show me off the best he could.

"They don't know about my past? Or, about our future?"

"There wasn't any need to tell them." He said simply. I looked to my mate with wide eyes of bedazzlement. I wasn't sure in that moment if he knew how much his actions had meant to me or not.

We'd been making the rounds but it was only when we moved around to my aunt and uncle that I realized they'd finally arrived. I hoped that meant that everyone else from my small list of guests had arrived as well.

"Aunt Mary, Uncle Liam. I'm so glad you made it." They smiled back before each pulling me in for their warm hugs. I took them in as they stood together dressed to the nines. My aunt had her dark hair all pinned in an updo. My uncle had on a dark grey shirt and black slacks. They made such a gorgeous couple but the cherry on top was the happiness radiating from them, bright as sunshine. I could only hope Caius and I were that happy in twenty years' time.

"We're just so glad to be here. The long-awaited day has finally arrived."

"We're so proud of you." And in my uncle's eyes I could see a deeper meaning. *My parents would've been proud too*. I knew that, but it made me happy to know that my family had still come to support me.

"How was your journey?" Caius asked.

"It was fine, would've been better if we'd sat Warren in between the two lovebirds." My uncles face took on a sour look while Caius chuckled.

"Speaking of the devils, where are my cousins?" I asked, glancing around to try and find them.

"Well you know Warren; he'll be scouting out the buffet table. I'm not sure where Lily ran off to but she brought

Scott with her. And I can only pray to the Goddess that they're not off making babies somewhere." We all laughed out at my aunt and her scolding look. Poor thing.

"Oh, Lorena! There you are. I must say you did a fantastic job with this shindig." My aunt ran off as soon as she spotted Lorena walking by.

"I guess we'll catch up with you guys later. Congratulations and we wish you all the best, dear." My uncle said befuddled at his wife, before running off after her.

We went back to greeting guests but after seeing my aunt I was itching like crazy to see my friends. I hadn't seen Carson since I left, and Dante when she had been rudely kicked out the night I went into heat.

As my eyes kept scanning across the garden hoping to catch a glimpse of them, Caius having noticed, released me into the wild. He must have felt sorry for me, pathetically looking like I wanted to be anywhere else. I pressed a grateful kiss to his lips before skedaddling off for a bit, leaving him to fend for himself.

I spotted Dante and her mother first so I made a beeline for their table. They had been holding martini glasses and toasting at the time. My arms wrapped around Dante from behind, "Guess who?"

"Ahh…" She let out a squeak and jumped from her seat to wrap me in a hug.

"Where. Have. You. Been?" She scolded me, waggling her finger in my face.

"Meeting and greeting. Ugh." I made a drab sound to follow the roll of my eyes, but still I held a gigantic smile on my face.

"Hey Allison, it means a lot to me that you came." I said after catching her eye.

"Thank you for inviting me Kira. It's been a lovely night out." She replies raising her half drained martini glass to me.

"Where's Carson and Tyler?" I turned my attention back to Dante.

"Hmm. They're probably still on the dancefloor." And so, to the dancefloor we headed. No more need be said.

We had a few dances together after finding Carson. To my surprise, she wasn't drinking and said they were leaving soon. I knew it was a journey back, which was why people had been invited to stay in the pack house or at one of the small B&B's in town.

"Carson and I haven't really seen too much of each other lately. We're both busy and it's just not been the same without you." Dante said as we sat down having a much-needed drink. After all that dancing, we were exhausted but in the best way. It'd been such a long time since we'd had a girl's night out, the last time was probably the night I was screwed over by Asher.

"I'm sorry I haven't been there for you Dante. But you know, you're welcome to visit whenever you like. I promise to try and visit too."

"I know, I know. I just don't wanna intrude. Not yet anyway, you two should stay in your little love bubble for as long as you can." She persisted. The thought that maybe she wasn't quite happy in Shadow pack crossed my mind and I made a mental note to bring it up sometime. She needed to know that if she wanted she could easily transfer over to us. I would've absolutely loved that, but her happiness took precedence over my wishes.

LUNAR ACCORD

With the festivities gradually dying down, I'd started making the rounds with Caius saying our goodbyes. I hadn't been around to meet the Elders but Cai did mention meeting with them tomorrow to discuss matters. Our destiny was not of a top priority on my mind right at that minute. I had spent the better part of my night watching Cai, waiting for the moment we could retreat. I had to admit I was feeling very ready to pounce on him.

"Cai, it's getting late." I squeezed his hand, grabbing his attention. I was ready, actually I was more than ready, I was restless and tired of this waiting game we had going on. I wanted him and I couldn't wait any longer. I refused to.

"Are you ready to go, my love?" He asked.

"I'm more than ready." My voice was low and huskier than I meant it to be but it worked in my favor to convey my lust even more. Caius' immediate response was to grab my hand and briskly lead me to his car, everyone else be damned.

On the ride home Cai told me all about the meeting he'd set up with the Elders for the next day. I had kind of hoped we'd have stayed in bed all day but I suppose we had to meet with them sooner or later.

Butterflies of anticipation began to fill my stomach as the car pulled up to the house. Everything had been so easy going until we made our way up to our bedroom. We paused outside our bedroom door, searing sexual heat spilling into the air. Grabbing Cai's hand, I held it in mine as I opened the door, pulling him in behind me.

"What were you waiting for?" I asked, genuinely curious if he had expected a written invitation or what.

"Nothing has to happen, you know? If you're not ready. We don't have to rush into anything, you know that, right?" His voice shook as he tried to talk me out of this, I thought that's what he was doing anyway. It was more than expected that Alpha couples consummate their relationship on the night of their ceremony.

I was stunned into silence as I looked at the man that in that moment, I realized I had fallen in love with. He was kind and supportive and loving, not to mention downright gorgeous. And in a rush, I suddenly wanted him to know. I'd never told him that I'd loved him before. *Why had I never told him? And why had it only just occurred to me that I had been feeling this way?*

"Caius. I...I love you." I whispered, gazing into his shimmering silver eyes.

"You don't have to say it back. It's okay. I feel your love more than words could ever express. But you need to know that I want you. And, I want to love you in every definition of the word." I rushed out as he stepped closer and closer. His lips rashly silenced mine in a sweet lingering kiss.

"I love you Kira. So much. I was waiting for the right time to tell you; I didn't want to be the first to say it in case you weren't ready to hear it."

CHAPTER SIXTEEN

I FLUNG MYSELF AT CAIUS unable to resist, unable to hold myself back any longer. The weight of my body pressed against his, my lips igniting a deep desire as they met his. They were home. The power of being the one in control, of being aware that his body was trapped between mine and the door, was hot as hell.

Our tongues fought as mine ventured and began exploring the depth of his mouth. I felt his bulge against my stomach as my hands timidly moved from his hair and started to roam his body. I pulled back to refill my lungs but continued to pepper kisses down his neck and over his jaw. My lips sought out his mate mark, licking and nibbling the sensitive spot gently. My right hand pinned steadily to his left shoulder using all my strength to keep him in place.

When his hands first made contact with my hips my knees wobbled at his tight grip that lit my skin with heat. He lifted me off the ground by my hips, my legs automatically wrapping around his body as he walked us backwards. I was nervous. *This was it, the wait was finally over,* I thought to myself.

Caius stripped me of my dress throwing it to the floor before making quick work of his shirt to follow. I sat on the edge of the bed with him looming in front of me. His rough hands gently gathered my long tresses moving them to lay over my shoulder. Sliding my bra strap down my shoulder his hand then moved behind me.

Over the past few weeks he'd caught quick glimpses of me in my underwear as I was changing. He was still yet to see me completely naked and as he tossed my bra across the room my breath hitched awaiting his reaction.

I knew I was beautiful despite what anyone said. I knew I shouldn't have been wishing that I could fix my flaws just so he wouldn't see them. I also knew it was silly to desperately seek his approval over my body. But I did.

Caius' silence unnerved me as he guided me to lay back on the bed. I kept my eyes trained on him as his hands skimmed up my thighs to my plain white panties. He paused, his eyes zoning in on my pantie-clad pussy. It was then that I knew that he'd seen it, my wetness. If I could feel it he'd definitely be able to see it. He released a sharp breath before continuing to tug my last single piece of remaining clothing down my body. I felt the bed jostle until I could feel his breath fanning my face.

"Open your eyes for me baby." He whispered into the still room. Opening my eyes, I saw his face hovering over mine. His hands were pressed into the bed either side of me holding his weight from me. His lips pressed soft kisses along the scar that marred the side of my face. Most of the time I forgot it was there until I looked in mirror and there it was staring back at me.

"You're so gorgeous Kira," His eyes were soft and a small smile graced his lips. He kissed my lips somehow

216

transferring his smile to my lips.

I was spread on my back looking up at Cai, my eyes followed his movements as he stood back on his feet. He unzipped his pants with a fierceness that I'd never seen from him before. Pushing his pants and boxers to the floor in one fluid movement I finally got to see Caius unrestricted for the first time ever. Stood in front of me like a reincarnation of a Greek god I greedily looked my fill.

His dark hair was a mess from my running my fingers through it. His skin was naturally tan, his muscles incredibly strong and toned. Rounded shoulders led to bulging biceps, vein popping forearms and big strong hands. His chest had a light dusting of dark hair over well-developed pec muscles. His abdominals were carved with deep ridges like nothing I'd ever seen before. He wasn't by any means lean or skinny, he was thick and ripped. Just taking in his upper body had my heart thumping, my need to touch him was rising.

My tongue darted out to wet my bottom lip and my eyes followed another spattering of hair that began at his belly button and led a trail down to his neatly trimmed garden. His cock, stood proud and tall against his belly, looked to be red with anger at keeping him locked away for so long. His thick prick leaked a glistening pearl drop that made my mouth water slightly. I definitely wanted a taste of him but I'd had a feeling that would have to wait until later. We had other things on our mind that took priority.

My eyes wandered farther down to finish off my thorough inspection of my mates naked body, his legs stood thick and strong with layers of muscle. He was sexy as fuck! Hell, I probably could've gotten off on just looking at him all night. But I was about to make him all mine, forever.

"I've waited so long to see you like this." He growled out his eyes scanning my body. Our eyes locked, heat rose to my cheeks as Caius parted my legs exposing myself to him and crawled up my naked body.

My arms wrapped around his neck and my legs around his torso. Leaning up to capture his lips I drew him into a long passionate kiss. I opened my mouth as Cai caught my bottom lip between his teeth, nibbling gently. His tongue plunged into my mouth with bold dominance before dancing with my own.

Pulling back Caius pressed a short kiss to my lips before starting to trail kisses down my heated body. He cupped my breast, kneading it, before trailing his tongue lightly around my nipple. The briefest of touches were causing such havoc on my body. I moaned softly as he finally took my erect nipple into his mouth. He grazed it with his teeth and I gasped at the desire that streaked straight to my pussy. His mouth disappeared from my nipple before swiftly latching on to the other.

After lavishing my breasts, his lips start to finally travel further south toward the junction of my thighs. The anticipation was killing me. He was being tender with me and I loved that but he was also driving my body crazy. As his lips pressed against my pussy for the first time my eyes rolled back at the little relief given to me.

I'd never had anyone's face so close to such an intimate area before. Being spread open before him was one thing but he was right *there*. I took a deep breath to calm my slight inner panic, his tongue did one long sweep of me turning my calming breath into a gasp of shock. It felt warm and oh, so good, like ordering a hot chocolate and it coming with extra whipped cream and marshmallows on top.

I moaned out when his tongue switched to drawing soft circles around my slit. I felt moisture start to leak from me, dribbling down my ass and to the bed. I could feel a warm tingling start to build inside me.

Concentrating on the budding sensations of my body, Caius started alternating between long firm strokes and quick circles around my little bundle of nerves. I rolled my hips towards his mouth, needing more. And he gave me more, picking up his pace until I couldn't take it anymore.

"That's it baby, cum for me." He groaned as the rubber band inside me snapped and I moaned his name and came on his tongue.

His fingers trailed up my inner thigh. The sensation giving me goose bumps before even reaching his destination. His mouth pulled away from my throbbing clit making way for his long fingers. He started swirling his finger pad in lazy circles around my slit. He then ran it down my wet folds to my entrance. With little force his finger was swallowed whole by my pussy slick with cum. I rode out my last waves on his finger, pulsing around him.

The room was silent, the only noise to be heard was us. Caius' heavy breathing, my marathon panting, our moans and groans combining and lingering in the air around us. When his finger started to move inside me my legs trembled still floating from pleasure. His fingers suddenly hit a spot in me that had my hands gripping the sheets. He added a second finger but continued to rub me. I fell over the edge of another orgasm as he sucked my clit into his mouth. I came on his fingers, squeezing them tight with pleasure seizing my body.

"You taste so good. I fear I'll never get enough of your sweet nectar." Caius groaned as he continued sucking me into his mouth.

Ready for the main event Caius stood to reach for the drawer of the nightstand. I knew what he was reaching for but something inside of me wanted to chance it. I wanted to throw caution to the wind, what was the worst that could've happened.

"Cai, don't. I mean…" I had no idea what I meant or how I'd explain it to Cai without putting pressure on him. That was the last thing I wanted to do, make him think I wanted children this very second. I just didn't want anything between us, I wanted to feel him unrestricted. Skin against skin. *Though*…"If it were to happen, I'd be okay with that."

I wasn't at a point in my life where I was desperate for children yet. But the thought of little Cai's running around didn't necessarily terrify me. I loved Caius, no matter what happened we'd be together and we'd be happy.

After a moment's pause, Caius' hand slowly retreated from the drawer handle. Something passed between our eyes, an agreement or understanding of some sort. I trusted him and he trusted me. Knowing that made my heart alight with warmth.

He positioned himself, ready to pierce through me with his big prick. I felt his unsheathed head bob against my wet entrance. Tilting my hips, I pushed towards him wanting more. He slid his tip up and down my slit teasing me, causing shudders to rack my body. I felt his pulsing need from just a brush of his cock and wondered how he was controlling himself. Looking up to his face I saw his eyes tight shut and his face pinched in seeming agony.

"Cai...I need you." My voice came out heavy and breathier than I intended but that only spurred him on more. After two orgasms, already my sensitivity was sky high. His hands slid from my waist to my hips as he rocked forward and pushed into me. He slid further in slowly allowing me time to adjust to his big cock stretching my inner walls.

I moaned loudly as he buried all of himself deep inside of me. After a pause filled with our erratic breathing he slowly pulled all the way out. He thrust all the way into me, our groans in sync as pleasure washed over us. His grip on hips tightened as his thrusts started to come faster and stronger. I rocked my hips to meet his, needing all that he was giving me. I cried out desperately as he slammed into me even faster and harder hitting a spot inside me that had my control slipping.

My legs wrapped around Caius as he came down on top of me. Wrapping my arms around him, I took joy in finally being able to feeling him against me. My nails ripped into his skin as I came for a third time that night. My legs tensed and my back bowed up off the bed, I cried out in pure ecstasy as I rode out my orgasm. My pussy clenched around his cock as he continued to pound into me. Only I second later is Cai twitching inside me, pouring his hot seed into me as he dropped off into his own sweet abyss.

Sweat covering us and cum leaking between us, Caius collapsed while we caught our breath coming down from our high. Our dazed eyes connected and I couldn't keep the smile from my face, I was absolutely spent but the happiness that shown from his eyes warmed my soul.

"I love you, Kira."

"I love you, Caius. For ever and always." In all my life,

I'd never felt anything so powerful but I knew it was only the beginning. We had a long night ahead of us and a lot of lost time to make up for.

That night we had sex, made love and fucked. And we did it until the sun came up and our sleepless night finally caught up to us. As Caius whispered words of tenderness to me and snuggled in closer, I fell asleep submerged in a moment of true bliss.

I woke a few hours later to Caius placing delicate kisses all over my face and body. I giggled once fully awake, only for him to stop and announce that he'd brought us breakfast. We ate our toaster waffles and discussed our meeting with The Elders that was scheduled for lunch time. Caius got ready and was the first to leave the bedroom as I continued to lie in bed.

I gave myself a moment to soak in last night. Never in a million years had I thought it would be that good, or that magical. Releasing a sigh, I sat up and made my way to the shower. As much as I really didn't want to wash away the evidence from last night that still clung to my body, I knew I needed to. We'd just have to replace the filth tonight.

I walked into the office to find everyone already sitting and chatting. Caius started the meeting shortly after I arrived and introduced me to everyone. Most of which I had met the night before. Among us were The Elders; Sebastian, Marcus, Xavier and Ariel. Trent was sat near the window, Cai's parent on the couch and his council were lined up against the bookcase.

Everyone settled down and Elder Sebastian was the first to have spoken. I was glad the home office had been larger than the one at the main house. I would not have been pleased to have been squished into that room with all these people, no matter how important the meeting was. "How much do you know of the prophecy?"

"Not much," Cai suggested rather cryptically. I was sure that everyone in the room knew of our prophecy, or curse, by now.

"All we read was the prophecy itself, it wasn't explained to us at all." I elaborated wishing the meeting would hurry up. If the Elders had such important information for us then why all the pleasantries and waiting around. They obviously knew something since they'd came all the way here.

"Well, 'Bound' mates are the Moon Goddess' redemption, so to speak." Sebastian continued.

"What does that mean?" Lorena asked, as curious as the rest of us.

"The Moon Goddess made a mistake when she paired you with Asher. You and Caius were born two halves of a whole. Light and dark, yin and yang. There is and always will be something inside of you programmed to seek each other out. Because things like this are so rare, Selene missed the connection."

"Selene created the prophecy to act as a guide for when you finally found each other, hoping for your forgiveness." Elder Ariel continued on to what Sebastian was saying.

"Okay, so what does the prophecy actually say then." I asked, my voice sounding shaken to even my ears. The longer they talked the more I worried for our future.

"Well, in basic terms, you're royal. You both only have a dormant gene, but when or if you conceive you will be bearing the first royal Lycan in over a century. You two are our one shot at resurrecting the royal Lycan bloodline."

My eyes darted to Caius.

Please tell me he's kidding, especially after last night. I thought to myself. The thought made me want to blush and giggle. But at the same time, I felt the need to run around the house screaming in a growing panic.

"Although, this part is less clear, the prophecy also states that resurrecting the royal hierarchy will bring peace to our lands. There's no how or when, unfortunately it's just said that when the light and dark greet the full moon together there shall be peace." Before he even finished speaking, my mind flashed to Caius' and my first and only date. That night we were stood under the full moon as we imprinted on each other.

"So, let me just get this straight. Our children will be destined to royally run all Lycan-kind?" I was in a state of shock; I couldn't wrap my head around it.

"They will have help from their council, but essentially? Yes, that's correct." He said. Like it was no big deal. On the contrary, it was a *huge* deal.

I was still breathing but I felt like my lungs weren't getting the oxygen that I was taking in. They were shutting down. I was shutting down. Was this what a panic attack felt like? I needed air. I turned and rushed from the room. I was no longer in control of my own body or my thoughts. I felt faint and dizzy while someone called my name from behind me.

I found the back porch then I felt myself flying and saw the grass growing closer. My eyes closed in fright before arms engulfed my body. From the scent, I knew I had landed on Caius. We lay there for a while as my heartbeat gradually calmed down. I took deep breaths as Cai held me tightly. Yet, his snug embrace was less restrictive than the panic that seized my lungs a moment ago.

"I love you so much Kira. I promise you, when the time comes we'll tackle this together." Caius whispered into my ear while his hand softly stroked my hair. His words helped to soothe my distress. I was scared, not for myself but for our children.

CHAPTER SEVENTEEN

A FTER CAIUS CALMED ME BACK down we returned to the office. The council had cleared out but Caius' parents and The Elders were still seated patiently. Lorena quickly pulled me into a tight bear hug and nudged me onto the couch next to her. I apologized to The Elders for my abrupt behavior but then I dazed off choosing to ignore the rest of their conversation.

To think that if I were to be pregnant at that very moment, I would've been bearing a royal child. A child that would one day be the ruler of all Lycans. It didn't feel real, which was probably why I still couldn't come to regret last night.

That night after changing my clothes I hopped into bed alone just wanting the day to be over. I was asleep long before Caius came to bed but I felt his warmth as soon as he crept into bed. He snuggled in behind me and I fell back into a dreamless sleep.

Time seemed to fly by as things returned back to normal.

It had been two weeks since our mating ceremony and it had been a busy two weeks. We'd been across to Shadow pack to visit my family, I caught up with Dante and I'd finally had that lunch with Mia. She'd gotten her mom to watch Sophie so we could head to the city. It was a much-needed girl's day out after having caught a bug that was going around.

Since our mating ceremony we had been on each other every night, nearly every morning and most lunch times. Caius and I had been on each other like rabbits which I found comically ironic. Last night he'd pounded away at me for three rounds, Cai was feeling particularly rowdy. By the time he'd tired out enough to get some sleep I was good and sore. We hadn't been able to keep our hands to ourselves. The fact that our children would be royals hadn't seemed to slow us down at all after that first night.

I was woken sharply sending my heart racing as I jolted up. A sense of Deja vu ran over me, my mind flashed to my mother rushing into my room about the attack. Immediately I reached out for Caius, who was already sitting up wide eyed and glaring at Trent and Oliver who stood in the doorway of our bedroom. Looking to the clock, the blaring red lights flashed just past one o'clock in the morning.

"What is it?!" Caius snapped out angrily. I reached over to stroke his arm hoping to soothe him.

"Alpha." They both quickly bowed their heads before Oliver started to explain the intrusion. "A rogue has been captured. I was running routine patrol on the western border when he approached me. We think he must have been travelling with others and we've being searching, but they must have run off."

"Where is he now?" Caius asked, tense and on edge at the very mention of rogues.

"In interrogation room four." Trent answered as Oliver shrunk into himself.

"I'm sorry to interrupt but, did you say he just walked up to you?" I asked while my brows furrowed in confusion. Was I hearing things, why in the world would a rogue wolf surrender themselves like that, let alone one that was travelling in a group. It had to be a mistake.

"Yes Alpha. I had absolutely no resistance when capturing him." Oliver answered.

"I'll be down in a minute." Caius said dismissively, compelling them both to leave the room.

Cai released a deep breath before throwing the covers off and getting up. As he disappeared into the closet I wondered if I should go with him, or if he'd even let me. Not really wanting to leave the warm bed, I decided I would stay put unless I was needed. Completely dressed and ready to head out, Cai made his way around to my side of the bed.

"Stay in bed, I'll lock the doors and I'm not far away if you need me. I'll be back in a little while." He held my hands in his, gently rubbing circles on my skin with his thumb.

"I know. And please, be safe Caius." I pulled him into a tight hug, one I didn't want to let go from. I knew that when I did he'd be on his way to a long stressful night, and I would be left to worry about him.

Checking the clock for the seeming millionth time, I saw it was only twenty minutes since the last time I looked. It was closing in on five o'clock. I huffed a loud agitated breath as I climbed out of bed. I'd been tossing and turning for hours ever since Caius was called away. It seemed I was not destined for sleep on that very night. Every time I heard the word 'rogue' I thought of Asher, this time being no different it had been plaguing my mind all night.

I got dressed planning to go find Cai once I was ready, little did I know that he was back and sitting in his office. His office door was open, the light on as I walked past on my way to the kitchen. Looking in I saw Caius sitting behind his desk looking like he wanted to tear his hair out.

"Cai? What's happened?" I hadn't even heard him come in.

"He had a message for you directly, we think that's why he was sent here."

"What was the message?" My brows furrowed as I wondered why rogues would ever want to be captured, they'd be tortured for information or otherwise killed instantly.

"He said…" Cai's throat is tight as he rubs his hands over his face, a sign that he's either stressed or angry. "The message was for you to be prepared to lose everything else."

I gasped in absolute shock, paralyzed slightly by the horror that ran through my mind in that moment. How had he found me? Had he been following us this whole time or did he have someone on the inside? Someone from my pack perhaps, or Cai's? There were only strict few from my uncles' pack and mine that knew I was still here, on Alpha Caius' territory.

"It's him," I spoke quietly but was confident that I was right in my accusation.

"I suspected it would be." Caius said through gritted teeth.

What did he want now? He took my family, smashed up my heart and sent my life spiraling down the toilet. Not to mention busting up my face, permanently scarring me. He must be one of those, 'If I can't have you, no one else will either' types.

My next words were spoken cautiously, trying not to upset my mate. "Cai, if he knows I'm here we may have a mole…"

The thought was upsetting but it could've been a very real possibility. He huffed and slowly nodded his head as if he didn't want to believe it either but agreeing it was a possibility. I felt sorry to doubt our pack members but it was a very likely scenario. It could've even been someone for my old pack or my aunts pack.

)) ◐ ◑ ◐ ◑ ((

A week after capturing the rogue, security had been tight and I was surprised when I opened the front door to Andrew.

"Hey stranger. What are you doing all the way out here? Are your parents with you?" Surprised to find him alone, me and Andrew had never been exceptionally close but it was a nice surprise all the same.

"Hey Kira. I thought I'd stop by for a visit. My parents aren't here but they did send you this." He held up a Tupperware container.

"Ok, well come on in. Want some coffee? I was just making a pot." I asked as I led Andrew to the kitchen.

"Yeah, coffee sounds great." He took a seat and I went about making us drinks.

"Caius just left to get some pack work sorted. I guess you heard about the rogue as well, huh? We've been crazy tight on security over here. I reached for the mugs from the cabinet and started to pour.

"How did you even get past the border? That must have been a nightmare." The mugs slipped from my hands as I turned back around. The ceramic mugs smashed on the floor splashing the hot black liquid everywhere.

Andrew stood behind me pressing something sharp into my lower back. "You have no idea."

I gasped in surprise both at Andrews outraging turn for the worse and that I hadn't heard him move. That wasn't the first time my hearing had dropped out like that either. "Andrew? What are you doing?"

"Sorry Kira. Just following orders."

"Kira!" I heard the voice of Mia called throughout the house. Andrew's head whipped in her direction and he quickly changed positions, wrapping his forearm around my neck pulling me closer to him. I eyed the knife in his hand that was pointed right at my neck. "Are you ready to go? I know I'm early but I thought tha-" Mia's voice cut short as she ambled into the kitchen.

"Andrew, did I mention I was going out to Brunch?" While he was distracting, thinking about how he'd possibly get out of this one, I threw my head back cracking into his nose.

His arm loosened around my neck as his other hand went to clutch his bleeding nose. I slashed my way out of his arm and spun around. My fist launched at his throat first then at his stomach. Bent over himself in pain he left himself open for my knee to drive up into his face.

He fell to the ground as I overheard Mia on the phone, "...She's kicking some guy's ass, there's no hurry just thought you should probably know."

Picking up the knife I held it ready for attack as I pressed my foot against his throat. Not hard enough to cut off his air supply just enough to keep him held down.

"Now that's how it's done. You need to teach me that." Mia said as I looked back at her.

"Can you check what's in that box?" I asked as I spotted the Tupperware that Andrew had brought in with him. I highly doubt it had cake or cookies in sent from Katherine.

Caius and Trent walked in through the back door at just that moment and I let up on Andrew knowing that they'd take care of him.

"There's a rag, a small bottle, and a black sack. Oh, he was so going to kidnap you." Mia answered as she emptied the container. Her arms wrapped around me as she started to freak out. I let her get it all out, I did owe her after walking in on us. If it weren't for her distraction I'm not sure how I would have gotten out of that one. He couldn't have made it far with me but the situation could have been a whole lot worse.

Caius was absolutely furious that I'd let him in, but I reasoned that I wouldn't have let Andrew in if I'd known he was going to try and kidnap me. He growled and huffed because I had a point.

))))) @ @ @ ((

Ever since Andrew had tried to kidnap me Caius had been tense. Of course I understood, but the extreme security precautions that he'd taken just seemed ridiculous. Andrew only got as far as he did because I had known him, grown up with him and his parents. He had the element of surprise on his side, but I wouldn't be blindsided by that again. Unfortunately, at this point everyone was to be watched, no one was free from a skeptical eye.

"Stay here. If you lose her, you'll be sent to the prison for a month before I exile you. Same goes for all of you."

"Cai…"

"Kerri-Ann, stay on her." He demanded. I almost felt bad for being turned on by his commanding tone.

"Caius." I called sternly. I'd shout the roof down if need be. Luckily for the roof he turned to me and stepped closer, I had his full attention.

"Where are you going?" I asked, I wanted him to be safe and close by in case anything happened.

"I'll be back tonight. I love you. Please, please don't run off, I can't handle anything more happening to you." Instead of giving him an earful about me being a strong independent woman, I gave him what I knew at this point he needed.

"I love you, Caius. I promise I'll be safe." And it wasn't technically a lie. I wrapped him in my arms and snuggled my face into his chest. He had to know that I felt terrible for worrying him. "I'm sorry all this is happening, Cai."

Caius had been in meetings strategizing all day. I knew he was scared, having been so close to losing me and that was his way of dealing with it. He'd been warning neighboring packs, enlisting the help of our allies and working with his council and warriors to up the pack security.

As I knew he was busy, I gave the four man, one woman security team he'd placed on me, a bit excessively

I might add, the slip. I packed a small backpack with makeshift tools that I'd need before lacing up my sneakers. Upstairs, I threw a ceramic lamp out the north facing window before quickly running and leaping out of the opposite window. The loud crash wouldn't buy me much time; the guys would be upstairs in no time searching for me. There was someone I needed to see and I knew Caius wasn't gonna like it, I just needed a head start.

I ran in human form heading south through the forest, past the pack house and down the hill. I hoped that my human form would somewhat dull my scent, making it harder for them to track me down. The field came into view and I wondered if my security team had told Caius yet. Or, were they playing smart and had coming out to look for me before informing Cai. They'd just about get their heads chopped off if he found out that they had lost me.

I took a second to swallow down the guilt as I dashed down the steps to the prison. I breathed in deeply, entering the code that opened both this door and the door to the Retreat, which was the fallout shelter used to house the women, children and elderly during attacks. Caius had given me the code right after we'd captured those two rogues in the case of any emergencies.

I tried to be as silent as possible opening the heavy bunker door. Slipping in, the guard station a few meters up ahead was manned by one guy. I crept closer, wanting to be as close as possible. As he turned back around to face me I lunged. It was Cregg, that sissy guard that had anger issues. I was cynically thankful it was him, payback was in the form of a five-and-a-half-foot Alpha Female and it would be a bitch.

My hands wrapped around his thick neck and held tight as I pinned him to the wall. Luckily for me he wasn't much taller than myself. His feet kicked and dangled as his face rapidly started to turn pink. One quick punch was all it took for Cregg to be out like a light. I dropped him to the floor and he fell onto his side. Most likely, he'd wake up in a little while with just a massive headache.

I walked through the door that led to the hallway lined with interrogation rooms. He'd be in number one at the far end of the row. I threw the door open with hefty force and scanned the room before stepping inside. I was not disappointed. Andrews limp, blood splattered body was hung against the concrete wall by silver chains opposite the one-way glass mirror.

"He's coming for you." He whispered. He knew it was me. I was immediately concerned at how strong his senses still were but that would be down to his bloodline. The chains holding him were pure silver, meaning they would not only have been excruciatingly painful but also draining his energy.

"I'm not too interested in that right now." I stepped past the threshold of the door and into the room. Shutting the door, I flicked the lock in place, I needed not to be interrupted. I wasn't worried that he was going anywhere, from the looks of the blood, he'd already been beaten.

I had loved and respected my father more than anything, so when he'd pulled me from bed and took me down to the prison cells as a child I trusted him. Those nights I spent with him watching as Noah interrogated countless Lycans and werewolves alike, I grew to know how it worked. I'd only used those keen skills once before, but never in a million years had I thought I'd be someday using them on Noah's son.

"I hope your father forgives me." His face took on a look of pure stupidity and confusion. I guessed that he didn't know that part of his father's job description. My father took great pride in teaching me how to be the best Alpha I could be. Often at times that meant showing me the dark things as well.

"Who sent you?" I grabbed the metal chair and moved it directly in front of Andrew, slipping my backpack off and plopping it besides me.

"No one." I pulled out the small household scissors from my bag, they weren't much but they'd do.

"Who told you to kidnap me?"

"No one." Reaching out, I ran the point of the blades along his exposed arm. Finding his vein, I bypassed it to a safe spot. It would hurt like hell but I didn't want him dying on me anytime soon. I held his arm steady as I drove the point into his arm. Blood droplets rained on me as he cried out.

"Who sent you?" I asked again drawing the scissors from his arm. I never liked watching interrogations, I liked doing them even less. I had always feared that the more you ripped someone apart, the more you learned to enjoy it.

"No one." He moaned out, his voice losing some of his conviction. And again, I jammed a fresh hole into his arm.

"I know who sent you. I know who told you to kidnap me. What I don't know is, why now?"

"Is it because I've found a new mate? Is this all just part of a plan to take over more packs and land?" His slight gruff didn't answer my question enough for my liking.

"Why now?" I gritted between my teeth, giving him another chance while slowly withdrawing the scissors from his upper arm.

His silence was all that was heard.

"WHY!" I reared back again before driving the file into his flesh, piercing yet another hole, this time just below his armpit.

"...to wipe out pack wolves." He rasped out.

"Pack wolves. To destroy the pack system...Why?" I hunched back into the chair to see him more clearly as I prepared to finally get some answers out of him.

"He wants to rule. He'll do whatever he can to get more power."

"What's he planning to do with all this power?"

"...enslave human kind." I laughed.

"He'd have to take over every pack nationwide. He'll never get past the east coast."

"Not traditionally. But maybe with a little roya-" He didn't finish his sentence as I stabbed my weapon with all my force, into the side of his kneecap.

I stood and paced around the room, the stench of blood hung thick in the air. So, he knew. That's what all this was about. But, I could only bear royal children with Caius. The real question was if Asher knew that or not. How safe was Caius in all of this?

"He will not touch my children!" I burst out with sudden emotion, determined to protect my pups.

"He's coming for you, so he can have them."

"And does, or does he not know that I can only breed children with Caius?" Again, the look on his face spoke for miles, telling me all I needed to know. Neither he nor Asher knew about that little clause.

"Also. There would be no possible way for me to get pregnant right now." *Because I heavily suspected I already was.*

As soon as I stepped out of the interrogation room Kerri-Ann was on me. Both hugging me to her and cussing me out. The four other guys appeared in the hallway, seeming to have emerged from the watch room. As they dragged me home with Kerri-Ann yelling at me, respectfully of course, all I could think was that I needed to see Caius. *Now.*

"Did you inform Caius of my being missing?" I interrupted Kerri-Ann mid rant, not that I'd been listening.

"We tried but he must have his hands full." She answered with a slight frown on her face making me think that something wasn't right.

It had been hours since we got back to the house. I had started to worry over two hours ago when it had begun to turn dark outside. Gazing out the of window as I paced back and forth, it was now pitch black outside and my worry had escalated into a full-blown panic. Asking the guards what was happening proved to be pointless.

Over the past two hours the guards had taken turns to come and check on myself and Kerri-Ann, and each time they'd quickly left the room with petrified looks on their faces.

Picking up the phone in Cai's office I dialed Trent's number.

"Trent! Don't you make me leave this house. You tell me what's going on right this second! If I have to leave this house to come and find you I'll be bringing your head back on a spike and roasting it for supper."

"We were ambushed."

"Trent! Where. Is. Caius."

"He's gone. They took him. I'm on m-" The phone dropped from my hand, clanging to the desk. I sunk to the floor. My heart shattered into a million pieces as tears flooded down my face.

They took him. Because they couldn't get me, they took my Cai. *He* took Caius away from me because *he* wanted me. I felt my soul folding in on itself until it gradually burned to ash.

CHAPTER EIGHTEEN

I DIDN'T KNOW HOW LONG I'd been crumpled on the floor like that but at some point, Trent had pulled me into his arms. His presence did little to comfort me but I appreciated the effort. My tears had dried up leaving my eyes puffy and irritated by the time sun light started to peak through the window. I realized I'd been there all night sobbing into Trent's shoulder.

"It was only me and him when dozens of rogues overthrew us. After, we tried tracking them but we didn't move quick enough." Trent whispered. The first words we'd said to each other all night.

"He'll be okay, Kira. We'll get him back." He continued on but his voice wavered and I had to question if he really believed that.

"We can't seem to figure out why they took him. If they wanted the pack they'd need both of you out of the picture. Which means they could be coming after you next. Although, they know we'll be expecting that. Never the less, I'll double your security, and I want you as close to me as possible in case anything happens." He mumbled on almost as if talking solely to himself, marking up his game plan.

I couldn't hold back the small throaty chuckle, "I think that's the most you've ever spoken to me."

"Huh. I guess it is."

"Thank you for wanting to protect me but I can take care of myself. And I'm not in any real danger just yet." At least not any physical danger, though my emotional state would be an absolute wreck until all this was behind us.

"Kira you can't know that." Trent shook his head softly.

"Actually, I can." I winced, "I went to see Andrew, I escaped the security team and went to the prison yesterday afternoon. I got him to talk."

"We already interrogated him, why'd he talk to you?" His brows furrowed making the tiredness on his face stand out.

"I have mad skills that you don't know about. And if that was him *after* being interrogated, you guys really need to step up your game." I was a girl and even I interrogated harder than that.

"He said that Asher knows about me giving birth to the royal bloodline. He plans to use me to his advantage in his plan to conquer the all packs. He doesn't want Cai. I suspect that he'll use him to draw me out, maybe try to make a trade." I explained hoping that I was right. The plan that was starting to form in my head would only work if Asher reached out wanting a trade.

"So, what do we do?"

"First things first. I need to see William." I couldn't do anything until I knew the truth.

Trent was pretty good at following along, he took me straight to the doctor's office without question.

I had been meaning to pop by the surgery for a week now, I just hadn't had the chance. But with everything that was going on, now seemed like the best time. I needed to know. If anything happened to me, I couldn't die without knowing.

William greeted us immediately and led us to a hospital room in the back seemingly away from everything else. I talked to William for a few minutes and watched as he went about conducting his little tests. I sat on the bed, Trent stood silently next to me as we waited for the good doctor to return.

"Well your suspicions were correct Ms. Brookes. You're not far along but you're definitely pregnant. Congratulations." Hearing those words without Caius by my side broke my heart. He had missed the moment. This wasn't how it was supposed to go, we were supposed to be together when we got told we were pregnant. We had talked about how we felt if it happened, he couldn't wait to have children, he had said whenever I was ready.

I was determined, now more than ever, to get him back. I took a sharp breath as did Trent. Looking to him I could see a small genuine smile dusting his lips.

"Congratulations Kira." He pulled me into a side hug before quickly releasing me. I hopped off the bed and thanked the doctor. He promised to keep it all confidential until we chose to announce it.

"What now Alpha-Momma?" Trent said with a small teasing smirk as we left the surgery.

"We wait. As much as it pains me, there's not much else to do. In the meantime, let's go take another visit to our prisoner. Maybe you'll learn how to interrogate someone."

We made our way across to the prison, punched in the code and stepped inside. I had on an evil smile as I spotted Cregg with another guard up ahead. He shook like a leaf as we made eye contact. I walked past him and to the interrogation rooms.

Opening the door to interrogation room one, I did a quick sweep before entering. Andrew wasn't so sharp today, he didn't notice my presence until I stopped in front of him. Looking back to Trent he shut the door and stood in front of it.

"Lock it." I said and watched as he flipped the lock. It was rule number one, never let yourself be open to interruptions. Being interrupted only made you look weak and out of control.

"Caius has been taken." I told him as I took a seat, he probably already knew that Caius was plan B.

"I didn't prepare today, so I don't have any sharp instruments on me. Answer my questions and I won't have to use my very dull, hair clip." I spoke calmly. Truthfully, I didn't come down to hurt him, I came to get answers. I didn't want to waste a perfectly good hair clip if it wasn't necessary.

"Asher will want to trade Caius for me, that right?"

"Yes." Andrew gritted out through clenched teeth.

"When?" I demanded harshly.

"Noon. He's not a patient person."

"How will he do it?"

"He…He'll come here. He'll want to kill everyone and take over after he has you." *Well duh. I hadn't expected us to trade off then hold hands and skip as we headed into the sunset.*

"Tell me something I don't already know." I was snappier then usual and I decided that I liked it. This side of me was such a turn on, I wondered what Caius would think of it. I hoped it wasn't just a pregnancy thing.

His eyes scatter around the room racking his brain for what to say. "He won't bring everyone if he doesn't think they're needed. He'll think this'll be an easy win because of how strong the bond between you and Caius is. He knows you'll never put each other in danger. So, once he has you, Caius wont attack, or vice versa."

"That's where he's wrong. We will attack, and I will retrieve Caius myself." My voice rose with determination. I *would* bring Caius home.

"Trent, could you bring him some water." I asked, wanting to reward Andrew for his cooperation.

The office at the pack house was filled to the brim. We were strategically planning what to do and what was going to happen when the office phone rang. We were all startled into silence as Trent picked up the phone. Looking at the clock it read just past eleven in the morning.

"It's for you." Trent said solemnly as he passed over the phone. We had anticipated this but he still wasn't happy about it saying something about how Caius would have his balls if happened to me. Whatever.

"This is Kira Brookes." I tried to keep my tone as natural and light as normal not wanting to tip him off.

"Kira. How lovely to hear your voice." I cringed, the last time I heard his voice he was rejecting me.

"Asher? What...How did you get this number? What do you want?"

"I have your precious Caius, I want to trade."

"What kind of trade?" I asked still trying to sound as innocent as possible. He didn't know me or what I was capable of, I then felt grateful that he'd never gotten to know me. I just hoped I'd fooled him.

"I'll let him go free but I'll need you to come with me instead. I'll even bring him to you myself." He said, like it was some great gesture that he was coming to overthrow our pack.

"Me? What do you want with me? Is he okay? How do I know he's still alive?" I wanted him to put Caius on the phone to see how he sounded, even though I knew it'd be painful to hear.

"Oh, he's alive alright but you'll just have to take my word for it." I knew he was alive. He was too valuable to Asher right now. Caius was the only way to get to me, he knew that.

"Where's the exchange?"

"The south-west corner." *What was in the south-west corner?* I thought to myself.

"When?"

"An hour. Oh, and Kira? Come alone." And that would be a big fat, *no chance in hell.*

"Not unless you do." I hung up on him sick of hearing his vile voice.

Looking up there was a pause before everyone started running around in a blind panic.

After calming everyone we packed our warriors up and

headed to the meet point. We got there early to scout out the area. He'd picked it specifically, for reasons unknown to us.

"Trent. Make sure you stay close." I said as the time drew closer to twelve and our wolves including Trent dove for cover. We'd had to make it seem like I was naively alone, only when the rogues revealed themselves would they.

Asher stepped out of the shadows, only seconds later his rogue wolves emerged around him. I was glad he hadn't stuck to our agreement; it'd make me feel less guilty for not sticking to it either.

My eyes zoned in on one of his men pushing Caius through the crowd, up to Asher. Clenching my jaw tight shut, I kept myself from crying out. Caius looked terrible, he was black and blue with silver chains around his hands to keep his Lycan from healing him.

"Trent," I whispered. It was time for them to come out of hiding.

As soon as our pack warriors revealed themselves the rogues charged. Both sides ran at each other and clashed together in a tidal wave of an attack.

Amongst the chaos I stood still across the field from Asher, I had to keep my eyes on him. His face had contorted angrily as he took in his outnumbered army. Grabbing Cai by the arm he shrunk back until he was once again swallowed by the trees and bushes. It was a trap but I had no choice but to follow him.

I walked across the field with Trent keeping a close pace as he slashed his way through rogue wolves. As soon as I stepped foot into his secret cave I was grabbed at by the throat. His tight grip on me held me in place. My eyes refused to meet his but instead sought out the spot on the ground where he'd thrown Caius.

My heart hurt as I took in my Cai, my prince. He looked to be in so much pain as he writhed on the forest floor. I once said I wouldn't trade Caius or our life together for anything. I was wrong. In that moment, I couldn't have disagreed with myself more. I'd trade him for myself. *I just hoped it didn't come to that.*

"I thought I said come alone?" His face had taken on a twisted angry look, the vein on his forehead visibly pulsing under his skin. *Maybe I wouldn't end up having to kill him, he might just have a heart attack before I'd even lain a hand on him.*

"As did I." I gritted out.

"It was so easy to capture him. Couldn't even defend himself." I stayed silent while he talked, I needed to buy some time until Trent caught up to us. I would need his help to free Cai before I took out Asher, otherwise it may've been too late.

"How is he gonna be when your pups come along? He won't be able to take care of them like I could, Kira." I thought I may have a screw loose because I was finding the garbage he was spewing hilarious. The only thing keeping my face sober was Caius, he'd began struggling harder against the chains since Asher had started talking. I was about ready to beg him to stop, he was only going to cause more damage.

"Just look at him, so weak." My eyes grew misty as they didn't move from Cai. My poor broken prince. His eyes were only just open, he looked bad. If we didn't get those chains off him soon I knew the effects would get more and more severe. Trent should've been close enough by now, we couldn't wait any longer.

He was trying to convince me to ran away with him, to leave my Caius. When in reality all he was really doing was throwing fuel on the fire. My Caius was not weak! I knew Cai and I knew he was strong and fearless and loyal. He was everything I'd wanted in a mate, and he was everything I wanted in the father of my children.

"Come with me Kira, we could rule the world. Together, as a family." His other hand stroked my belly and a built up rage broke over me. I harshly brought my knee up to Asher's groin, it was a high school move but it was a classic for a reason. He groaned and fell to his knees.

"Trent!" I screamed out, knowing he wouldn't have been far behind. The thought that he'd touch my baby belly made me sick. I heard a loud grunt before the bushes behind me shook and Trent appeared.

"Help Caius. *Now!*" I hadn't moved as I commanded him to get the silver off of Caius' body.

My eyes closed, finally taking a moment away from the sight of Caius. The longer I had looked at him the sadder I became, and that made me even more furious.

My attention turned and zeroed in on Asher, the scum of a man struggling to get to his feet. I threw my knee up into his face causing him to fly backwards. Once he was on the ground I grabbed at his collar. I dragged him back through the trees and threw him onto the field. This was going to happen, and I wanted everyone to see it.

The last time he attacked, I was human, of course he'd had the upper hand. Now, well he was as good as dead. He shouldn't have come here but I was glad to have gotten the chance to finally kill him once and for all. He messed with my mate, in turn, messing with me. And everyone knew you didn't mess with an Alpha-Momma.

"Get up!" I screamed at him. The loud growl that followed out of my mouth reverberated around the clearing. My canines extended, my nails grew and fur started to cover my body. I was trying to hold myself back but my Lycan was seeping through the cracks as I was about to explode.

"Shift." I snarled, my voice coming out more wolf than human. I was surprised I was still holding my human self together. Asher shifted, his reddish-brown wolf standing up tall and ready for a fight.

Inhaling a deep breath, I let the rage take control; my body shifting and growing with it. Landing on my front paws I opened my eyes to the difference between us. My wolf was a whole head taller than him, he wasn't anything special and I was guessing that as he stood there he was just figuring that out.

I let out a fierce snarl before lunging at him. I wouldn't even give him a chance to try and save face. This would be unlike any other fight. I wouldn't be humoring him; I would be going straight for the kill the first chance I got.

I snapped my jaw at him trying to get to get a good angle on his neck. His paw tried to swipe at me, I caught it between my teeth crushing bones. I let it fall from my mouth before swinging my paw at him, his beastly body twisted to the side on impact. I took the opportunity to hurdle my body at him, throwing my weight against him.

Asher's wolf crashed into a nearby tree. As he got to his feet I rammed into him again causing the tree to creaked. By now I'd noticed that the wolves surrounding us had stopped fighting to stare. I backed off and let him get up. He stepped forward, in my direction, limping slightly.

Out of the corner of my eye I caught sight of Caius. He

was free of the chains but he had Trent under his arm helping him to walk. Our eyes connected and I sighed out of relief. My Cai would be coming home tonight; he would be okay.

I heard a whoosh of air and turned my head just in time to see Asher launched in the air. I kicked my legs out against his belly as he landed on top of me. He flew off of me just for me to climb on top of him, pinning him to the ground. I looked into his eyes before snapping my jaw at his neck. His howl died in his throat as I ripped it out. The taste of his blood filled my mouth as I threw his skin down. My teeth bit down and shook until his head had dislodged from his body.

Shifting back into my human skin, I was very much naked but dripping with the blood of my ex. Everyone around me had come to a halt to watch as I tore through Asher, *Leader of the rogues*. Oliver was quick to be by my side, handing me clothes to pull on. My eyes rose from where Asher's body lay to the wolves still left on the field.

There were a few rogue wolves lying dead, the rest had been injured and scattered. Running off with their tails between their legs. We would have to deal with hunting them all down, one by one, and killing them off. We had to make sure they didn't rebuild their forces, but that could wait for another day. As I stood above Asher's body I gripped his head in my hand and lifted it in the air for all the see.

"VICTORY!" I cried loudly. Our Lycans erupting in applause and grunting. I dropped the head as Caius stepped up behind me.

"Let's head home, I think I've just about had enough excitement for a while."

I seriously hoped he was joking. How was I supposed to drop it on him that he was going to be a father? As much as I wanted to spill the beans on the battlefield, I thought Lorena's method would work best.

Everyone dispersed, there would be meetings held tomorrow but for the afternoon everyone was released from duty. Caius and I headed home for a much-needed bath and first aid kit. I'd helped him walk all the way back to the house but it wasn't until we got to the staircase that I wished I had of taken Trent up on his offer to help.

As we got to the bedroom we both collapsed to the bed. I was certain that I was out as soon as my head hit the pillow. It wasn't until dinner time that I woke up wondering where the time had gone. Reaching out the bed was still warm but Caius was no one to be found. Getting up I wandered the house until finding him in the kitchen.

He was by the stove stirring a pot of what looked to be mac and cheese. My eyes grew moist before they started leaking tears onto my cheeks. I stood in the archway of our kitchen, just watching as my mate, that had been beaten and broken only hours ago, hovered over the stove cooking us dinner.

While his clothes were fresh I knew he hadn't showered yet. He still looked so much better. His bruises had almost completely vanished, he was walking perfectly and even his coloring had returned to normal. That sleep seemed to have done him a world of good. Being finally freed from the silver chains had let his body recover at his usual Lycan speed.

"Hey." He turned and caught sight of me across the room, "You hungry?"

"Cai?" I stepped closer needing to be in touching range.

"I have something to tell you."

His face dropped in two seconds flat, "I know he was right in saying those things about me."

"What?"

"I'm weak. I doubt how I'll ever be able to protect you if I couldn't even protect myself."

"Really? You were up against dozens and silver chains. There is nothing you could've done. *Hell!* There's nothing anyone could've done." I wrapped my arms around his waist, gripping his chin between my fingers. "You are one of the strongest people I've ever meet. And not just physically Cai, mentally too."

"I love you, Kira."

"I love you too, Cai. For ever and always."

"If that wasn't it, what did you have to say to me?" His eyebrows furrowed cutely as he remember that it was me that had wanted to speak in the first place.

"You'll be strong enough to defend me. And you'll be strong enough to defend our pups. Don't ever doubt that." I wrung my hands together, suddenly very nervous that he'd freak out about my news.

"Kira?"

"I went to see Dr. Tate. He had some news for us."

"What is it? Are you okay?"

"I'm pregnant Caius."

He froze, his eyebrow raised, staring holes into me. I gave him a couple minutes to digest and come out of his shocked state.

"You, you're pregnant?"

"We're pregnant Cai. With our first pup. I know it's probably not the best timing and all tha-" His lips crashed into mine, smothering all my doubts and insecurities. His hands gripped my hips, lifting me into the air and twirling me around.

"You good with this?" I asked as I pulled myself back from his intoxicating lips.

"Kira, I'm fucking amazed with this!" His megawatt smile showcased his pearly whites, his face was alight with happiness. Reaching my arms around his neck I pulled his face back to mine. Our sweet celebratory kisses soon turned heated. Gripping my ass in his hands he gave a squeeze as he walked us out of the kitchen and upstairs to out bedroom. He put me back on my feet as we started stripping our clothes off. I grabbed his hand and led him to the bathroom.

Shower sex wasn't something we'd tried before; we had always been in too much of a rush. I turned on the tap and waited for it to heat up. Cai's kisses had continued up and down my neck as his hands ran across my nonexistent baby bump.

"I can't wait to spend forever with you." He mumbled into my neck.

"Let's not focus on forever right now, let's focus on the next half an hour."

Caius let out a sexy growl as he backed me into the shower, stalking towards me. Cai showered me with his kisses, his love and affection, and his happiness. My legs shook from all that he had rained down on me. I didn't know it was possible to feel dirtier coming out of a shower than you did going in. It was the best shower I'd ever had.

EPILOGUE

One year later...

IT HAD BEEN A YEAR since Caius had been taken. I thanked the Moon Goddess every damn day for getting him back to me. I just knew I wouldn't have survived without him. The bond between Caius and I had only grown stronger each and every day since I'd got him back.

Being pregnant hadn't been easy. Caius had been a nightmare at some points. He'd treated me like crystal, ready to break if I'd stepped too suddenly. I spent the nine months arguing with Cai that, yes I could do the dishes and no I didn't need a nap. I had tried my hardest to keep in mind that he was being sweet.

Three and a half months ago, after twelve very painful hours of labor, I gave birth to our beautiful baby girl. She'd barely ever been out of our arms since. She'd brought so much joy and light into our lives that Caius was already thinking up names for our next one.

Caius said she looked just like me and that she would grow up to be strong and independent just like her mother. I only hoped she had her fathers' heart of gold.

Lorena and Phillip were daily visitors, not being able to go long without seeing their granddaughter. Uncle Liam and Aunt Mary weren't much better; they'd been over to visit nearly every weekend since the birth. But, to my complete shock, it was Trent that had taken to her the most, he couldn't hide his special bond with her. Our little girl had certainly charmed the pants off of everyone.

Our baby girl. Our little princess was to grow up famous amongst our kind, to eventually become our next ruler. I worried everyday over her safety but The Elders had sent down the best warriors we could've hoped for. I knew that as long as Cai or I were close by, that nothing would happen to her.

She would be protected and loved by our family, our friends and our pack. We would all stand by her as our baby became a princess. She would grow up, meet her mate and then become queen. I could only hope that she didn't have as much trouble with her mating as I did mine.

I watched out the bedroom window as Caius sat on the rocking chair on the back patio holding our baby girl. The sight was so precious that it had me glued to my spot not wanting anything to disrupt the moment.

We were the proud parents of the little Lycan Princess, Zoe Lynn Matthews.

AUTHOR'S NOTE

Dear Readers,

As I have enjoyed writing Kira and Caius' magical tale so much I hope to bring you a sequel sometime in the near future. It is on my list of things to do, along with a million other things. If you're interested in being kept updated on what I'm working on and my new releases head over to my social media pages or simply email me.

Twitter: *@AuthorCMcDonald*

Instagram: *@AuthorCMcDonald*

Facebook: *www.facebook.com/pages/AuthorCMcDonald*

Email: *authorcmcdonald@gmail.com*

I'd like to give a shout out and an unbelievable thank you to my book bestie, Hannah, for being an absolute gem on this (very long) journey. We finally made it! I hope you'll never quit your full-time job as my therapist, editor and idea bouncer, not to mention trusted friend.

A massive thank you for reading Lunar Accord. I hope you enjoyed my very first novel as much as I did. And if you did like it, I welcome you to write a review on amazon to help promote the book to other curious readers. Plus, I very much wanna hear your thoughts and feedback.

Until next time,

Chelsea xo

Printed in Poland
by Amazon Fulfillment
Poland Sp. z o.o., Wrocław